A DANGEROUS INVITATION

"How would you like to become one of us?" Ashlyn asked, turning suddenly toward Kimberly. "A Predator?"

Ashlyn McConnel was one of the richest and prettiest girls attending Cooper Riding Academy. If there was anyone in this school with whom Kimberly would have gladly traded places, it was Ashlyn.

Kimberly was tired of being pushed around by other girls. The idea of having even a shred of the power Ashlyn wielded appealed to her immensely. "What do I have to do?"

"There's an Initiation."

For a moment, the two girls stared silently at each other. Kimberly noticed the hardness in Ashlyn's eyes.

"I don't mean to seem ungrateful," Kimberly said finally, "but why me?"

"Maybe because I was like you once and someone helped *me*. Maybe there's a *lot* of reasons . . ."

•

NOW OPEN!
THE NIGHT OWL CLUB

Pool Tables, Video Games, Great Munchies,
Dance Floor, Juke Box, *Live* Bands On Weekend.

* * *

Bring A Date Or Come Alone . . .

* * *

Students From Cooper High School,
Hudson Military Academy,
Cooper Riding Academy for Girls
Especially Welcome . . .

* * *

Located Just Outside Of Town.
Take Thirteen Bends Road,
Or Follow Path Through Woods.

* * *

Don't Let The Dark Scare You Away . . .

* * *

Jake and Jenny Demos proprietors
Teen club, no alcohol served.

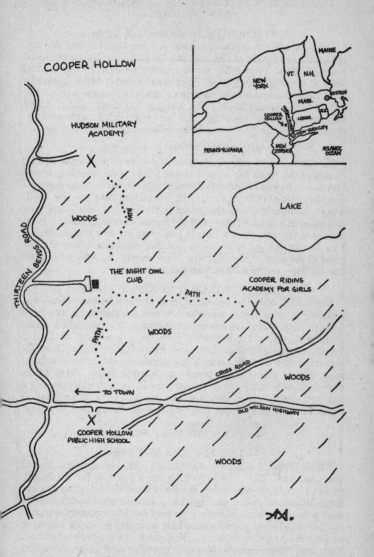

COOPER HOLLOW

MAINE

NEW YORK
VT. N.H.
MASS. BOSTON
COOPER HOLLOW CONN. R.I.
NEW YORK CITY
PENNSYLVANIA NEW JERSEY
ATLANTIC OCEAN

HUDSON MILITARY
ACADEMY

X

THIRTEEN BENDS ROAD

WOODS

PATH

LAKE

THE NIGHT OWL
CLUB

PATH

COOPER RIDING
ACADEMY FOR GIRLS

X

WOODS

PATH

CROSS ROAD

WOODS

TO TOWN

OLD WILSON HIGHWAY

X

COOPER HOLLOW
PUBLIC HIGH SCHOOL

WOODS

#2: THE INITIATION
Nick Baron

Z·FAVE
KENSINGTON PUBLISHING CORP.

Z*FAVE BOOKS are published by

Kensington Publishing Corp.
475 Park Avenue South
New York, NY 10016

The Nightmare Club series created and edited by Alice
Alfonsi.

First Printing: August, 1993

Printed in the United States of America

For Denise

Prologue

She was seventeen and beautiful. The midnight wind blew her hair into her face. The moonlight caused her skin to glow pale white, her dark eyes to reveal a passionate yearning.

He loved her. As they embraced in the clearing, surrounded by powerful trees whose gently swaying branches seemed to lean in to hear his words, he whispered that he would love her his entire life.

A rustling came from somewhere close. He started, looked around sharply, and drew her into his arms.

"Don't be afraid," she whispered.

"I heard something."

"It's all right. I told you I had a surprise for you."

He looked into her lovely face and was instantly set at ease by her warm and slightly mischievous smile. "I thought maybe you were followed," he said. "I thought it could have been one of The Chalmers' Patrol."

"No," she said. "Don't worry. I've been careful."

She was a Junior at the Cooper Riding Academy for Girls. Elise Chalmers ran the school. Curfew was strictly enforced by her staff. Nevertheless, the beautiful young woman he had fallen in love with had managed to sneak away on a regular basis to see him. For this, he felt like the luckiest boy in Cooper Hollow.

"It's time," she said softly. "Do you want your surprise?"

Pulling her close, he kissed her once more. "Yeah, I want my surprise." He shook her playfully, his powerful arms wrapped around her slender waist. "Gimme,

gimme, gimme!"

She laughed. "I brought something for you from Cooper."

"Show me."

She held his hand tightly and guided him deep into the woods along a narrow path he had never before noticed. Suddenly, they came upon a magnificent gray horse tethered to a sturdy pine tree. He gasped, his mind unwilling to comprehend the incredible sight.

When he was a child, his family had owned a farm in Virginia. Much of his early childhood had been spent on horseback. When he was nine, the banks drove his parents out. His family moved to Cooper Hollow so that his father could go to work in his brother's insurance firm in the city. Adjusting to life away from the farm had been difficult. For years, he had felt crippled by the loss of his daily rides. When he imagined once again climbing on the back of a sturdy mount, he nursed a phantom torment, as if from a limb that had been painfully severed.

He wanted desperately to tell her that he had never seen a horse so powerful, so majestic. But he knew that if he tried to speak, he would cry. Instead, he squeezed his girlfriend's hand, parted from her, and took a few cautious steps in the animal's direction. Its massive head swiveled around and he was caught by its warm and inviting gaze.

"Come on," his girlfriend said with a wide, amazing smile. "Let's go for a ride."

Nodding, he took a few moments to run his hand over the horse's flank, and eventually allowed it to lick his hand. Pressing his face against its mane, he hugged the animal, then came around and mounted it as if only minutes, not years, had passed since he had last been astride a horse. He watched as his girlfriend untethered the horse. When she was finished, he held out his hand and she climbed on behind him, encircling his waist with her lean but very strong arms, the arms of a horsewoman.

"I know another path," she said. "Once you've got the feel—"

"I love you," he said.

"You, too," she whispered.

With her guidance, they found the path. He had already become attuned to the gray horse's rhythms, and felt comfortable with the animal, confident that it would respond to his every command. He wanted to urge the horse to break into a run, but that would be too dangerous. After they cleared the woods outside the school and reached the bank of the lake, then they could be a little more reckless. For now, they would continue to navigate carefully the tight channels between the closely bunched trees. He was grateful for the advice his girlfriend whispered in his ear. The woods were a labyrinth and he would have been lost without her.

Suddenly, the gray horse stopped.

"What's the matter, Beauty?" he asked. With chilling slowness, the creature turned its head in his direction. Its eyes had become crimson. They blazed, slicing through the darkness like the tips of hot pokers poised to run him through. His instincts told him to dismount instantly, but before he could do so, before he could even speak a warning to his girlfriend, the animal bolted forward. All he could do was put his head down and hug the neck of the creature. He prayed that his girlfriend would not panic. She held onto him as they barreled through the woods. Low-lying branches reached for them, threatening to swipe them off the back of the charging mount. The boy restrained a scream as a skeletal branch grazed his arm, ripping a bloody furrow in his jacket.

The trees they passed on either side seemed a blur. The wind whipped the mane of the gray horse into his face and he was almost overcome by hysteria as he felt the soft hairs tickling his face. The itch that resulted was so terrible he would have done anything short of releasing his grip on the animal to scratch it.

11

He could feel the beat of a thundering heart pounding against his chest and had no idea if it was his heart or that of the horse. The creature's flesh, however, once hot and vital to his touch, was freezing. His fingers began to tingle, as if he were clinging to a block of ice and might suffer frostbite if he didn't loose his hold.

Still, the boy held on.

Suddenly, with a final rustling like the parting of a veil, they burst through one last thicket of trees and were out of the forest. Now they were racing along the shore of a sparkling lake. The boy's efforts to bring the gray horse under control failed miserably, and his relief at escaping the deadly woods was short-lived. The animal was, impossibly, gaining in speed. The wind kicked against the boy's face and he had to turn his head slightly. The itch was still driving him insane. His only source of comfort was the feel of his girlfriend's arms around him. He had to protect her. Nothing else mattered, not even his own life.

Without warning, the horse came to a full stop and reared up with a cry that was unlike any sound the boy had ever heard. It was a shrill, murderous noise.

The gray horse bucked and tossed the riders into the air. The boy felt his girlfriend's hands come away from him as they were wrenched from the animal's back. A splash sounded somewhere to his left an instant before he himself struck the icy waters. Then he was in the murky depths, struggling to reach the surface.

Suddenly, his head rose above the water of the lake. He was free, he had survived! His feeling of exultation faded quickly. The horse was gone and there was no sign that his girlfriend had reached the surface. She might not have been thrown so far into the lake; she might have struck her head on a stone in a more shallow part of the water.

Without hesitation, he drew a deep breath and dove under the lake's black surface.

It was the last breath he would ever take.

She waited on the shore. The gray horse stood beside her. She had seen her boyfriend's head emerge briefly. He had looked directly at her, but he had not seen her. Nor had he seen the horse beside her, its flank cold, its fetid breath turning immediately to steam, its red eyes glowing in the darkness. She turned from the creature so that it could not see her tears.

Only a few bubbles marked the spot on the lake where her boyfriend had gone under for the last time. She knew what he had seen and felt. The strange tugging, then the sight that illuminated the darkened waters; the sight that was enough to drive any mortal insane with its varied and hideous aspects.

Suddenly, a blackish-red geyser spouted from the surface of the lake. Blood and bits of bone rained down, then were immediately sucked below, far below, to the maw of the creature the girl served.

"Goodbye," she whispered. She was about to add, "I love you, too," when a remarkable sensation coursed through her. The change that had been promised had been enacted. It was shocking in its swiftness. She was glad that she had not spoken those final words to her dead boyfriend. The Sentinel beside her would have interpreted those words as weakness, and rightly so.

She had passed her Initiation. The fear and regret she felt at the sight of her boyfriend's passing had vanished in an instant, replaced with a numbing sense of purpose, and the first, vague stirring of a remarkable power. Promises had been made to her. She now knew that those promises would be kept. The power she had been told about was *real*.

"Come on," she whispered, turning away from the lake. She did not wait to see if the Sentinel would follow her. It moved behind her as silently as a shadow. "We have a lot to do . . ."

13

One

Five months later.

Kimberly Kilpatrick unlocked the door to her private room and went inside. She was wearing her full riding habit — tan riding pants with matching jacket, a white shirt, and black knee-high boots. Her brunette hair had been braided and hidden beneath her black riding helmet, which she now removed and tossed on the bed. Kimberly was trim and only five-foot-three inches tall; nevertheless, the manner in which the seventeen year-old held herself was striking. Kimberly seemed impervious to any outside force. Nothing was farther from the truth.

Kimberly's room at the Cooper Riding Academy was considerably more austere than her room at home. Kimberly went to her plain dresser and opened the middle drawer. Two photographs lay within, one of her real parents, who had died when she was very young; the other of her uncle and his wife, her guardians. Until four months ago, when she had enrolled in Cooper's summer riding classes, Kimberly had lived with them. Now their picture was only brought out when she knew they would be visiting.

The photograph of her real parents meant infinitely more to Kimberly. Carefully, she took it out and looked at it. The reassuring smiles of her mom and dad always made her feel better, no matter how horrible her day had been. In her room at her guardians' house, Kimberly kept entire photo albums devoted to her parents. Her uncle hated when she dragged them out. David

15

and Margaret had not wanted the responsibility of raising a child. Kimberly knew they resented her parents for dying and leaving them with such a burden.

When Kimberly had suggested attending Cooper for her senior year, her aunt and uncle had leapt at the opportunity. What a relief that had been. Anything would be better than living with her unloving guardians, or so she had thought at the time.

Kimberly had been an honors student at her last school. At Cooper, she was barely making the grade. She carried five subjects and had at least four hours of homework a night, more on weekends. Recently, she had fallen into the habit of staying up half the night to work with a penlight after "lights out" had been called.

Then there were all the rules of conduct she had been forced to learn. At Cooper, a lapse in protocol was treated like a capital offense, and her rich, snobbish classmates reveled in reminding her of her mistakes. The teachers were pleasant, but severe. Only Jane Hadrick, the assistant headmistress, had been kind enough to take Kimberly aside and guide her through the complexities of her new existence.

Kimberly entered the school as a senior, and that had entitled her to many privileges. But resentment was high from the lower grade students. They had been laboring for years, looking forward to the day when they would have the right to walk on the grass instead of the gravel, the day they would be allowed to step onto the senior staircase, the day they would be treated with awe and respect. Kimberly had just walked in and had it all handed to her.

Those who had come up through the ranks and were Kimberly's "equals" were even harder to handle. In their opinion, there was no such thing as a school that equaled Cooper; the school Kimberly had transferred from had been a *public* high school, for heaven's sake, and her uncle was not even registered in *Who's Who*, the *Blue Book*, or the *Social Registry*. The man's law practice had made him wealthy, but there was wealthy and there was *fabulously wealthy*. Kimberly's uncle simply didn't make the grade, and, therefore, neither did Kimberly.

Still, there was one major advantage in Kimberly's becoming a full-time student at Cooper — the opportunity to ride several times a week. The only time Kimberly felt true freedom was during those precious hours when she was astride one of the academy's powerful mounts. In all her life, *nothing* had ever spoiled that experience. Not until today, at any rate.

Sharon Cruise, a girl who hated Kimberly with a true passion, talked her father into purchasing the one horse with whom Kimberly had bonded. And Sharon had reserved the pleasure of passing on this information to Kimberly for herself.

Kimberly attempted to show no reaction. She was determined not to give Sharon the pleasure of seeing her tears. But now that she was safely back in her room, holding onto the photograph of her true mother and father as if it could protect her, Kimberly threw herself on her bed and wept openly. Lightning was the closest thing Kimberly had to a friend at the academy. Now even he was gone. It was always the same. Everyone she loved went away.

After a while, Kimberly's tears slowed and she began to think. It *could* be worse, she realized. Though she was considered a reject, it was not as bad as having the honor of being *the* reject, the one that was marked for the year-long "Rite of Passage." Another girl, Thelma Hopkins, had been given that honor. Each year, one girl was picked to bear the insults of all the others: to serve them, to be humiliated by them, and to lose all hope of ever being accepted as their equal. Kimberly had been told various horrible stories about the ritual during which this title was bestowed.

From what Kimberly was able to piece together, a girl was taken from her room, with her mouth taped up so that she couldn't scream, and a pillowcase thrown over her head so that she couldn't see where she was being taken. When the girls arrived at the destination, the pillowcase was removed from the victim's head so that she could see her surroundings — usually some dark, smelly place, possibly a furnace room, and packed with dozens of her classmates. She would be forced to perform rituals — maybe act like an animal. Then she would be beaten and her hair would be chopped short to indicate her new station. Then the girl was warned that if she made any attempt to tell Ms. Chalmers or the other teachers about what had happened, she would be severely punished.

To date, not one of the girls who had been marked for the "Rite of Passage" had made it through the entire academic year without transferring to another school. But that was all part of the plan. Only the girls who were hated the most, those whose presence was no longer desired, were given this treatment.

Kimberly wiped away the last of her tears. She felt guilty at being relieved that someone else would suffer this fate. *No one* should have to go through anything like the "Rite of Passage." Still, with all of her own problems, she could not help but be grateful that she had not been targeted for this "honor."

Kimberly found herself beginning to relax. The past week had been hellish. Waiting for Sharon's next prank or punishment had made her tense. Its arrival had almost come as a relief.

No, that wasn't right. She could not allow herself to be relieved at the thought of Lightning in the hands of Sharon's family. Her parents seemed oblivious to their daughter's faults. Sharon had probably whined and pleaded with her daddy to buy her the horse but now that she had him, Kimberly was sure she'd neglect him terribly.

The spoiled little witch, Kimberly thought. Sharon would grow tired of the animal soon enough and her parents would sell him to someone else, certainly at a profit.

Rising, Kimberly left the photograph of her parents

on the bed and went back to her small dresser, where her stuffed bear from her childhood sat. It was a silly blue bear with a big white stomach. She touched its smiling face. Her parents had given her this bear. Or, they had meant to, anyway.

Kimberly thought again of the day on which her parents had died. She was a child, a day away from her ninth birthday. She had spent the entire Saturday afternoon in her parents' restaurant, playing as they labored to get the place ready for the dinner rush. She remembered that she had hounded them, begged them to tell her what gifts she would be getting for her birthday.

At one point a ball she had been bouncing off the wall behind the building had fallen down the basement stairs. She chased it underground where she smelled something funny.

Kimberly retrieved the ball and went back upstairs. She remembered being about to tell her father about the smell, when she spotted a shiny blue bicycle in the middle of the restaurant. Her mom and dad stood beside it, grinning from ear to ear. Tom Kilpatrick said, "We thought we'd give you one present early."

All thoughts of the terrible smell had been driven from her head. She laughed and squealed excitedly, and was overjoyed when her mom told her to go outside and try it out.

Kimberly had taken the bicycle out of the restaurant and was two blocks away, pedalling as fast as she could, when a muffled bang sounded from the direction of her parents' restaurant. Kimberly stopped the bike. Turning, she saw a black cloud of smoke rise up into the air like an angry fist. Kimberly raced back to the restaurant, but it was too late. The place was on fire. She tried to run inside, but one of the people in the crowd that had sprung from nowhere grabbed her and hauled her back.

Years later, Kimberly learned that what she smelled in the basement was gas. If she had warned her parents, they might have gotten out of the restaurant alive.

But she had been thinking only about her wonderful new bicycle. Her parents had paid the price for her greed.

If only I could see you, Kimberly thought, her fingers running over the furry belly of her little blue bear. It was one of the other presents her parents were going to give her for her ninth birthday. Tears welled in Kimberly's eyes.

"I wish I could talk to you one more time," she whispered. "Tell you I'm sorry. Say goodbye."

She picked the bear up and hugged it to her. Then, she frowned. Something was horribly wrong with the stuffed animal. It was heavy and it *squished* as she pressed it tightly against her chest. She was dimly aware of a cold, wet substance leaking down her arms. When she looked down, she saw something that couldn't possibly be real.

With a scream, Kimberly dropped the bear. It struck the floor and exploded with a muffled *plop*. The seam that had been holding it together tore open and a grotesque collection of blood-drenched intestines and internal organs splattered onto the floor. Blood was on the front of her uniform, on her hands, her arms.

Kimberly felt ill and choked back her urge to vomit, aware that she would raise her bloody hands to her mouth to do so, which would make it all the worse. Belief in what was before her came slowly. She felt light-headed and dazed.

This can't be happening, she thought. No one could do something like this. It wasn't human.

Suddenly, she heard the door to her room swing open. Apparently, she had not closed it all the way. It would have locked if she had. Someone was in the room. Hands were on her arms. Kimberly was turned away from the sight of her precious little blue bear, her bleeding little blue bear. A regular drip of crimson came from its small bow tie, which read, "best friends."

"Oh God, oh please, no," Kimberly muttered. Her mind was not ready to accept anything like this. How

20

could anyone have been so cruel?

Then she realized that more than one person had entered the room. At least five girls had crowded in. One of them carried a white pillow case. Kimberly recognized two of the girls as Sharon's friends.

She tried to pull away from them, but it was too late and there were too many of them. Her hands were yanked behind her back with enough force to cause Kimberly real pain. Kimberly saw Sharon leaning casually in the doorway, arms crossed, a wicked smile on her lips.

Sharon laughed. "It just hasn't been your day, has it, Kilpatrick? Look at it this way: Because of you, at least one person is going to have a good year after all."

Kimberly's heart felt as if it might explode as she heard the awful rip of packing tape being pulled apart. Before she could scream, a patch of sticky tape was secured over her lips. An instant before the pillowcase was brought down over her head, Kimberly saw a short, fat, red-haired girl standing behind the others. She did not share the malicious glee of the other girls. Instead, her expression revealed an uneasy mixture of terror and relief.

It was Thelma Hopkins.

Oh, God, Kimberly thought, it's me, I'm the reject this year, not Thelma after all. Visions of the year-long "Rite of Passage" flashed into her mind. They were driven out as Kimberly remembered her parents' photograph lying on the bed.

Please, God, don't let them see it. Tell them to leave it alone. Please!

Then she heard laughter and the tearing of paper that could be nothing but her tormentors ripping her precious photograph to pieces.

21

Two

Kimberly was dragged through the corridor. Four girls held her, one on each wrist and ankle. She wanted to cry out, but the tape prevented her from making any sound other than a muffled cry of terror. Images of the humiliations she would soon face flooded into her mind.

Where was Mrs. Alcott, Kimberly wondered. She was the adult monitor assigned to this floor of the dorm. Had they created some diversion? Bribed her? Drugged her?

The procession stopped suddenly. Kimberly guessed they were at the end of the corridor, about to descend the stairs. They had stopped only to adjust their grip. After all, it wouldn't do to drop her down the stairs and bring damaged goods to the "Rite of Passage."

"Put her down," a voice said.

The voice was that of another student, not Mrs. Alcott.

"I thought we had an understanding," said a voice Kimberly recognized as Sharon's. "I don't interfere with you, you don't interfere with me."

"Put her down," the other girl repeated simply.

Kimberly was amazed to find herself gently deposited on the landing at the head of the stairs. The unknown girl commanded, "Take off the pillowcase and the tape."

At once, the soft cloth was pulled from Kimberly's head and she saw the face of her savior. The girl seemed familiar. She had auburn hair, deep blue eyes, and a magnificent figure.

Ashlyn McConnel—one of the richest girls attending the academy. If there was anyone in this school with whom Kimberly would have gladly traded places, it was Ashlyn. The beautiful girl had the ability to take control of any situation. She seemed unfazed by the stresses of the school, somehow above it all no matter what was going on.

Kimberly had never spoken to Ashlyn. She had it in her head that Ashlyn was stuck-up, not unlike her tormentor, Sharon Cruise. Kimberly wondered now if she had been wrong about Ashlyn; the compassion Kimberly saw in her eyes could not be denied. Then Ashlyn looked back to Sharon, who stood above Kimberly, and the hardness returned to her gaze.

"Finish it," Ashlyn said.

Sharon reached down and yanked the tape from Kimberly's mouth with such force that it stung horribly. Nevertheless, Kimberly was grateful to be free of the restriction.

"This girl is under my protection," Ashlyn said forcefully. "If anyone goes near her again, she answers to me. Is that understood?"

The girls who had joined Sharon scattered at the sound of these words. Only Sharon remained to face Ashlyn. They were silent as they stared at one another. Finally Sharon turned away from Ashlyn's fiery gaze. She vanished down the corridor, following her friends.

Kimberly scrambled to her feet. She was going back to her room to pack. Ms. Chalmers could call Uncle David and Aunt Margaret to come pick her up. Nothing was worth this terror. Nothing.

"Hey," Ashlyn said. "It's all right."

Kimberly dully registered the girl's voice. She could not bring herself to believe Ashlyn's words. *Nothing* was going to be right again, not so long as she stayed in this place. She had made a mistake; she had to get away from here. No matter what, she had to get away!

"That's *not* the way," Ashlyn said. "If you start running now, you'll never stop."

Startled, Kimberly looked back at Ashlyn, who gestured at her bloodied clothes. "We've got to get you out of this stuff," Ashlyn said. "Take me to your room."

Kimberly nodded. They went back to her room and Ashlyn helped Kimberly undress. After Kimberly's blood-soaked clothing had been removed and piled up in the corner of the small, adjacent room, Ashlyn found a towel and helped Kimberly rub away the worst of the blood. When they were through, Kimberly's flesh felt raw, but it wasn't enough. She could still feel the blood on her.

"Throw on something dark and go use the shower," Ashlyn said. "Go on. I'll take care of all this."

Kimberly hesitated. The reason for her concern was evident to Ashlyn, who placed a comforting hand on her shoulder. "Sharon won't go anywhere near you. Believe me."

Kimberly did not want to leave the safety of Ashlyn's presence. Suddenly, memories of Ashlyn's unnatural command of the other students raced through her thoughts.

She believed Ashlyn.

Kimberly crouched down and pulled a suitcase from beneath her bed. In it, she had packed blue jeans and several sweatshirts. One was black and she slipped it on.

As she stood, she saw what could only have been the torn remains of her parents' photograph. The pieces sat on a heap near the edge of the bed. She caught sight of her mother's smiling face ripped down the middle and immediately looked away.

They had to tear up *this* one, Kimberly thought bitterly.

"You'll be here when I get back?" Kimberly asked.

"I'll be here. Don't worry. It'll be like none of this ever happened. I promise."

Shaking, Kimberly nodded. Her eyes began to drift to the side of the bed, where the bear lay. Ashlyn stepped in front of her, guiding her to the door.

"Don't look back," Ashlyn said. "Just go."

Kimberly left the room and heard the door close and lock behind her.

Three

Kimberly took a steaming shower, scrubbing her flesh until it felt tough. Before long, the gore that had clung to her was washed away.

She went back to her room and knocked on the door. She felt odd. This was *her* room. Sharon had gotten into it somehow and had done the terrible thing to her little bear. Then Sharon's friends had burst in and taken Kimberly and she had been powerless to stop them. Now someone else was in her room and she had to knock for entry. This wasn't right.

Ashlyn opened the door and Kimberly walked inside. The blood was gone. Ashlyn had been as good as her word. Then Kimberly noticed something sitting on the edge of her bed. She went to it and snatched it up, her heart racing.

It was the photograph of her real parents. The girls had not torn it up after all! But she had been *certain* that it had been destroyed.

"I found that on the floor," Ashlyn said. "I had the feeling it meant something to you."

Kimberly looked back to the bed and saw the torn remains that she had glimpsed before. The picture of Uncle David and Aunt Margaret had been destroyed, not *this* one. Kimberly nearly laughed out loud. It didn't seem possible, but she wasn't going to think about it any more. She had her photograph. That was all that mattered.

"Happy?" Ashlyn asked.

"You can't imagine. What did you do with my b—" Kimberly bit off her own words when she caught her

25

reflection in the mirror above her dresser. For an instant she saw herself covered in blood. She blinked, and her reflection was normal. The illusion, probably a product of her worried mind, was all she needed to recall her rage.

"I'm going to get Sharon thrown out of Cooper for this. I'm going to tell Ms. Chalmers. She'll get that witch out of here so *fast*," Kimberly said, suddenly aware that her nails were biting deeply enough into the flesh of her palms to draw blood. "I can't *wait* to see Sharon's face."

"Do you really think they're going to do anything to her, even if you do tell?"

Ashlyn was right. Shoulders sinking, Kimberly whispered, "Great. So what can I do?"

"Maybe together we can think of a better way of getting back at Sharon," Ashlyn said softly.

Kimberly looked down and ran her hand over the photograph. The image of her true parents calmed her. "There's something I don't understand."

"What's that?"

"Why are you bothering to help me?"

Ashlyn frowned. "If you don't *want* my help, I'll leave."

Before Ashlyn could move, Kimberly's hand closed over the other girl's wrist. "I'm sorry."

"It's all right. You must be pretty shook up."

Kimberly nodded.

"And I know what my reputation is in this school. Do you know what they call me and my friends?"

"Yeah. 'Beauty's Daughters.'"

"It's from a poem by Byron. 'There be none of Beauty's daughters with a magic like thee; and like music on the waters is thy sweet voice to me.' Pretty, isn't it? Now tell me what they *really* call us."

Kimberly felt uncomfortable, but she knew this wouldn't be the first time Ashlyn heard the term. " 'Predators.' "

"*That* name was *my* idea."

26

"Why?"

"Why do you think? I got tired of being pushed around. Sometimes the only safe place is at the top of the hill, looking *down*.

"It's how you see yourself, Kimberly. If you see yourself as a victim, then you're going to *be* a victim. If you think you deserve *this*, what Sharon did to you, then you're opening the door to more grief. You're just giving the bullies of this world an invitation to come in and walk all over you. You've got to take what you want in this life and you've got to know in your heart that you deserve it. You *have* to believe that or nothing else matters.

"Now get dressed. You can't go out looking like that again."

Kimberly glanced down at her sloppy attire. The school had a strict dress code. Putting her photograph on the nightstand, she went to her closet, picked out a new uniform—plaid skirt and vest, pastel colored blouse, low-heeled shoes—and quickly dressed. When she finished, Ashlyn was standing before the dresser, looking down at the spot where the bear had sat. She strummed her fingers on the hard wood.

"How would you like to become one of us?" Ashlyn asked, turning suddenly. "A Predator?"

For a moment, Kimberly didn't think Ashlyn was serious. Then she saw the hardness in Ashlyn's pretty eyes. Kimberly *had* been pushed around long enough. The idea of having even a shred of the power Ashlyn wielded in this school appealed to her immensely. "What do I have to do?"

"There's an Initiation."

Kimberly stiffened. Images of the hazing from which Ashlyn had just rescued her seared into her brain.

Ashlyn smiled slightly. "It's nothing bad. When the time is right, we ask you a question. If you give us the right answer, you're in. If you don't, you're out."

"That's all?"

"That's *plenty*. You haven't heard the question."

27

"When do you ask the question?"

"When I think you're ready."

"I'm in."

"That remains to be seen," Ashlyn said wryly. "But I'm glad that you're interested. I think you'll make a very good candidate."

For a moment, the two girls stared at each other silently. "I don't mean to seem ungrateful," Kimberly said finally, "but why me?"

Ashlyn shrugged. "Maybe because I was like you once and someone helped *me*. Maybe there's a *lot* of reasons."

"Thank you," Kimberly said in a small voice, attempting to suppress the emotions welling inside her.

Ashlyn smiled. "Let's get some dinner."

Kimberly looked quickly to the photograph of her true parents. She thought she should put it away. What if Sharon or one of her friends came back . . .

This girl is under my protection. If anyone goes near her again, she answers to me. Is that understood?

Smiling, Kimberly left the photograph on the nightstand and followed Ashlyn out of the room.

Four

They did not encounter Sharon as they passed through the maze-like corridors of their dorm, Beacon Hall. The main building of the Cooper Riding Academy for Girls had once been a grand hotel, as towering, Gothic, and sinister as anything in Stephen King's *The Shining*, or so Kimberly had often thought. Ms. Chalmers, the headmistress, had her own house on the property. Another building, which had been the servant's quarters, was used to house some of the teachers and horse handlers. The animals themselves were kept in a luxurious barn three quarters of a mile from the school's main building. Nearly a dozen surrounding buildings were used as classrooms, gymnasiums, and dormitories. A guest house was perched away from the school. At the far end of the property, not too far from one of the riding rings lay an old graveyard. It, like everything else at Cooper, *including* the students, was fenced in.

Kimberly's first thought when she had seen Cooper months earlier had been of a military compound. She had not been surprised when she learned of the strict regimens the students were expected to follow. Their every moment was accounted for, from the time the registered aides woke them by prowling the halls at six-thirty in the morning, ringing loud and piercing bells, to lights out at ten-thirty at night.

Dark was slowly approaching as Kimberly and Ashlyn reached the main building. The meal times at Cooper were as strictly regimented as every other aspect of the students' daily lives. Three times a day the girls were lined up outside the dining hall and allowed to enter single file. They were expected to take their seats without breaking the code of silence. When the last student was seated, permission was given for the girls to talk freely among themselves, provided they remained orderly and kept their voices at an acceptably low level.

Kimberly followed Ashlyn inside. Two girls joined them. Ashlyn briefly explained Kimberly's situation to her friends. The girls smiled warmly and Kimberly felt at ease.

Each dining table seated eight. One girl sat at the head of the table, the other, at the foot. Three sat on each flank. The girl at the head of the table was the server. Her task was to gather the meals and distribute them at her table. The girl at the foot of the table had the job of clearing the table when the meal was finished. These positions rotated nightly.

Kimberly, Ashlyn, and their two companions were the only ones at their table. When the signal came for the servers to rise and come to the kitchen, a girl from another table came with a small notepad and took their selections. She kept her eyes down and spoke nervously.

The dinner choice was meatloaf or veal. Kimberly chose the veal, surprised that she had any appetite left after the ordeal she had just endured.

"I feel like I'm in *The Godfather*," Kimberly muttered when the girl had walked away.

"Is that bad?" one of the girls asked. "I'm Nikki," she continued. "This is Tanya."

Nikki had midnight-black hair and bangs that ended just above her eyebrows. Her eyes were sharp green; her cheekbones, a model's; and her lips, full and red. Excessive makeup was frowned upon at Cooper, and it took Kimberly a moment to realize that blood-red was the natural color of Nikki's lips.

In contrast to Nikki's full figure, Tanya's was boyish. Her long blond hair was braided; her skin was pale;

her eyes, soft and blue. To Kimberly, she seemed either bored or distracted.

"Hey, 'Vito' Kilpatrick," Ashlyn said. "Look at that."

Kimberly turned and saw Sharon staring at her with a look of hatred laced with fear.

"See?" Ashlyn said. "Hanging out with us has its advantages. And it's a hell of a lot better to be the Predator than the prey."

"I'm curious," Nikki said. "Exactly what happened between you and Cruise to make her hate you this much?"

Kimberly had no reason to hide the truth from these girls. "It was the first week I was here. We were both in the parking lot, behind the school. I didn't see her, she didn't see me. All of a sudden there was this crash. I spun around and saw Sharon standing next to Ms. Gilchrist's car with a brick in her hand. She had busted the side window. Must have gotten a grade she didn't like or something. One of the assistants came running out and Sharon freaked.

"Sharon saw me and told me to take the blame for it. I told her 'no way' and she got mad—told me she'd make it up to me later, to just do it. But I wouldn't. She nearly got expelled. Her father got her out of it, of course. She's been doing things to me ever since."

"Don't worry," Ashlyn said. "We have plenty of time to deal with her."

"Yeah," Tanya said, her gaze fixed on a spot on the far wall. "Sometimes it's better to let a meal simmer for a while before you eat it."

Tanya's words were delivered with a coolness that both alarmed and excited Kimberly.

"So, are we still on for Wednesday?" Nikki asked.

"Sure," Ashlyn responded. "It's my anniversary with Greg. There's no way I'm going to miss it."

Nikki laughed. "Think he'll remember?"

"Our one year anniversary?" Ashlyn asked. "Hell, no. He probaby doesn't even remember that I caught him with his tongue down that girl's throat last week."

Kimberly recoiled. Nikki responded with a knowing smile. "If this guy's so rotten to you, why don't you break up with him?"

"He's gorgeous," Ashlyn said simply.

"Yeah. Too bad he knows it," Nikki answered. "Well, it's always good to get the hell out of the prison."

"So, it's true," Kimberly blurted. "I heard that you guys have a way out of here. Look, I don't mean to be the voice of reason or anything, but what about studying? Maybe this school is easy for you guys since you've been here a few years, but it's not for me. I went to a public high school before Cooper and they didn't make you work like *this*. I feel like all I do is stare at books, and if I don't keep up my average, I'm not going to be back next semester."

"Exactly the reason to break out of this prison," Nikki said. "Work hard, play hard. If you don't, you'll crack under the pressure."

"Seriously," Kimberly added nervously, "I might get kicked out if I don't start doing better in class. I can't afford to be wiped out."

"You don't *have* to come with us if you don't want," Ashlyn said. "Just think about it."

"All right," Kimberly said. "I will."

"I'm sorry about what happened to you," Tanya said in her distant voice, still staring off into space. "I had some stuffed animals when I was a kid. I was like, I dunno, ten? Whatever. My brother's four years older than me. Y'know, mature. Or at least, he's supposed to be.

"I had this one stuffed animal. A little dog. Axelrod. He was like my best friend, but he was getting old. You could kind of see the stuffing coming through his seams. I loved him, anyway.

"One day, my brother and his friend Karl kidnapped Axelrod and sent me a ransom note, all the words clipped from newspapers and everything. I was all upset and they thought it was hilarious. Then I thought of something. I went into his room and took two of *his*

32

stuffed animals that he had from when he was a kid, and I sent *him* a ransom note.

"He got really upset. He was mad. All he kept telling me was that I wasn't playing fair. Nice, huh?"

"What is your *point?"* Nikki asked in exasperation.

Tanya refused to look away from the spot on the wall. Her eyes were bright, her smile filled with malicious glee. "Sharon Cruise reminds me of my brother. I think she needs to be taught a lesson. I think she needs to see how it feels to be on the receiving end for a while. How does that sound to the rest of you?"

"Wonderful," Kimberly whispered.

"I'm in," Nikki said. "I could use some entertainment."

Ashlyn surveyed the faces of the other two Predators and smiled. "Kimberly, I think you're a hit."

Kimberly walked through a field she had never seen before. A lacy white gown clung to her. She was aware that it was bitter cold, but the fires of her own excitement warmed her.

A few yards away, a horse stood waiting. It was not Lightning. Her precious friend was gone forever. The animal poised before her was sleek and gray. She patted its flank and ran her hands through its wild mane. Its eyes were hard, nightmare-black. This did not frighten her. She climbed astride the animal as if she had been riding it for years. The mount brooked the familiarity stoically. Horse and rider shared a common goal, after all.

Kimberly issued a command and the horse bolted forward. She was not afraid that it would go out of control, or that she would fall off. The horse would protect its mistress from harm. An unspoken pact had been made. The terms of their understanding had been negotiated with a single look.

The wind whipped her hair into her face and she shouted with triumph as she tossed her head back. Suddenly they were in an unfamiliar woods, passing through a maze of low-lying branches. Dark, skeletal fingers attached to sweeping arms rose up on every side of her. Kimberly laughed. It would take more than this to frighten her.

Suddenly, she became aware that they were not alone in the woods. Just ahead, stumbling through a clearing, was a girl Kimberly's age. She was tall, with dark, flowing hair.

Sharon.

The girl's terror was evident. The gray horse raced after Sharon, and Kimberly did nothing to stop it. She giggled as Sharon fell before the horse's hooves, laughed as her tormentor was trampled beneath the creature.

Kimberly woke suddenly, startled. She was in her room. The door was locked and she had propped a chair underneath the doorknob, just in case. The clock beside her bed read five past two in the morning. She was covered in sweat, breathing hard.

Kimberly reminded herself that it had just been a terrible dream. Sharon was alive and well.

It was only a dream.

Kimberly knew her dream was real but she was no longer certain that she was comforted by that fact.

Five

Kimberly and Ashlyn devised a plan for getting back at Sharon and they implemented that plan swiftly and without mercy. It began on Tuesday morning. Ashlyn learned Sharon's schedule and made certain to position Kimberly and herself wherever Sharon had to go. They said nothing to the girl. Merely smiled.

"Loser," Sharon hissed as she passed Ashlyn and Kimberly one last time before dinner. Though she held herself with righteous indignation, her hands were shaking.

Dinner was a covered dish. When Sharon removed the cover to her meal, she found the bloody entrails she had packed into Kimberly's bear. She screamed, dropped the cover back down on the plate, and ran from the room. The adult monitors chased after her, caught her, and brought her back to her table to explain her outburst.

Sharon was nearly hysterical as she pointed at the dish, shouting that she knew who had done this, that it was that "little Kilpatrick tramp." When the monitor picked up the lid, all she found was the meal the server was supposed to bring.

"I'm going to kill you for this!" Sharon wailed, pointing at Kimberly. *"I'm going to kill you!"*

Sitting beside Kimberly, Ashlyn muttered, "Not likely."

The next day, Sharon arrived at class only to find the pages in her three-ring binder replaced by blank sheets. The binder had contained all her semester notes and homework. At riding practice, Nikki bumped into

Sharon by "accident" and drove her face down into a stinking pile of manure. When she went back to her room after taking a shower, she found all her uniforms and casual clothes missing.

That night, Sharon's fitful sleep was shattered as a rock crashed through her window. She fled, woke Mrs. Alcott, and dragged the woman to her private room. The rock was gone. The glass had not been broken. Mrs. Alcott told her it had been a nightmare, nothing more, and crossly ordered her back to sleep.

Kimberly had no idea how these pranks were being accomplished. When she asked Ashlyn, her new friend only smiled and told her that explanations would spoil everything. Kimberly agreed.

Wednesday morning was the best. Kimberly had the satisfaction of dogging Sharon's every move. She giggled as Sharon — suffering from lack of sleep — nearly walked into a wall. Her bloodshot eyes darted about nervously. She evidently was coming to understand how it felt to know that no one was on her side. Kimberly knew that feeling well. She wanted Sharon to get used to it.

Finally, just before lunch, Sharon approached Kimberly and said, "I want it to stop."

"It stops when I say it stops," Kimberly replied shortly.

Sharon shuddered. Her mouth twisted into a sneer, and Kimberly could tell she was about to make some kind of threat — a threat they both knew she couldn't back up. Instead, she lowered her head and said, "I'm sorry."

"Excuse me?" Kimberly said, so delighted by the words of her former tormentor that she could hardly stand it. "I don't think I heard that."

I'm sorry, Sharon repeated, now nearly shouting the words.

"For what? What did *you* ever do?"

"You know what I did."

"Tell me."

36

Sharon rattled off a list of her crimes. Though the confession took some time, Kimberly was still disappointed. Seeing Sharon humbled and humiliated like this *should* have been enough for her, but, for some reason, it wasn't.

"I'll get Lightning back, if that's what you want," Sharon said, nearly crying. She had been popular, nearly as popular as Ashlyn and her friends. That had only been a few days ago, but it might as well have been another lifetime.

Kimberly looked over at Ashlyn. "What do you think? Think she means it?"

"I dunno. Hard to tell." Ashlyn frowned. "It's not really enough, is it? I mean, all things considered."

"No. But it's a start, I suppose."

"Then you'll lay off," Sharon asked desperately.

"Maybe," Kimberly said playfully. *"Maybe* I'll consider it. For now, though, a girl's just *got* to have fun."

With a "kiss, kiss" motion, Kimberly turned and left Sharon behind.

"I don't understand!" Sharon cried. "I don't understand! I told you everything! I'll do anything you ask. Tell me what you want, I don't understand!"

Once Kimberly and Ashlyn were out of Sharon's view, they broke into hysterical laughter.

"How did that feel?" Ashlyn asked.

"Good," Kimberly said with a giggle. "So good, I can't even begin to tell you."

"I understand. Believe me, I remember how it feels."

Kimberly shook her head and hugged herself. "It's wrong, though. It's *wrong* to feel this good. I know that. It's just—for some reason—I don't really care. I've just been through too much to *really care.*"

"Well," Ashlyn said, "you're in charge. Any time you want this to stop, you just give the word."

"I don't know if I'm ready *yet.*"

"That's fine. Have you thought any more about our little adventure tonight?"

Kimberly nodded. "I've been thinking about it a lot.

It's like what Nikki said, 'work hard, play hard.' I need to get out of here and the weekend just seems too far away."

"Great. I'll knock on your door around eleven. Be ready to go."

"I will be," Kimberly said, exhilarated. "I can't wait."

Six

Kimberly felt like a child being guided through a wonderland of endless corridors, shadow-laden chambers, and rickety old stairs. Ashlyn and her friends had taken this route many times. They knew which hallways would be monitored. They had memorized exactly where to place their feet on the old wood stairs to avoid making them creak. Two adult attendants were on duty; the first of these, Mrs. Alcott, had a room at the end of the first hallway and kept her door ajar. Mrs. Alcott swore that she was a light sleeper and would be jolted awake by the slightest noise. If anyone was about performing mischief, they would be making a mistake by passing her door, and they would *have* to pass her door to get to the stairs.

Mrs. Alcott slept like a rock. The slight laughter of her companions and the sound of their footsteps did not even make her twitch.

Sneaking around like this was something Kimberly had never done before. She had always been a good girl, coming home before curfew and obeying her aunt and uncle's house rules. But the regimented lifestyle at Cooper was far more stifling than any rules and restrictions her guardians had ever placed on her, and she was certainly ready to break a few of them. She felt giddy as she followed her new friends through the darkness.

Her nerves jangled as they passed through the music room, where bizarre shadows were cast by the misshapen forms of the abandoned instruments. She shook with anticipation and fear as she navigated the final corridors separating them from freedom.

"The horses," Ashlyn said simply.

Kimberly nodded. A group of figures darting across the greens might spook one of the animals, and the sounds of the horses' wild panic could give them away. As they slipped beneath a section of the fence that had been clipped in places to allow passage, Kimberly clenched her teeth to such a degree that her gums ached and her jaw felt sore after she finally relaxed. It didn't matter. For a short time they were free. That was worth *any* price.

By the time they had reached the woods, Kimberly's legs ached. She was well aware of the mud on her shoes and jeans and wondered how she would get them clean. It would have to be done when she went home for the weekend in two days. Until then, she would be careful not to allow Ms. Chalmers' agents to see them. Jeans were not to be worn on the school grounds. Kimberly kept hers as an act of defiance. She usually wore them only when locked in her room.

They walked for twenty minutes, reached the edge of the woods, and found a black pick-up truck parked with its headlights on. A black-haired guy wearing a white tee-shirt and torn denim jeans stood in the glare of the lights, puffing on a cigarette. His long, wolf-like face was set in a scowl. He wore his straggly hair in a ponytail, though strands had escaped and fell in his face. His eyes were small and dark and piercing.

"Took you long enough," he said. His voice was coarse and raspy.

Kimberly was not at all impressed. The boy was pretty — perhaps prettier than she was — and he knew it.

Ashlyn ran to him and tried to embrace him. Frowning, he held her at arm's distance until he was able to take another puff. Then he dumped the cigarette and kissed her.

Kimberly's cool immediately faltered. She may have believed herself to be tough, at least in theory, but the sight of this boy plunging his tongue down Ashlyn's throat embarrassed her terribly. She had had several male friends, but none of them were actual boyfriends. Boys had asked her out, but her uncle had made it clear that she was not allowed to date and she had followed his rules, no matter how antiquated and unfair they had seemed to her. She had been kissed a few times at dances, and once, in the parking lot behind the high school she used to attend, but these were stolen moments shared with awkward boys.

Ashlyn's boyfriend was anything but awkward. He knew exactly what he wanted and he took it. Kimberly could almost understand Ashlyn's attraction to this young man. His brash, animal nature was frightening—and exciting.

"I wish you wouldn't smoke so much," Ashlyn said as she pulled away from him. "It's like kissing an ashtray."

He laughed, dismissing her words and her discomfort. "You're not happy unless you've got something to complain about. I bet your new friend over there wouldn't mind. She looks like she's gone too long without getting any."

"You're a real pig," Tanya muttered.

"Real nice," he said. "Like I *have* to be here picking you girls up. I could just take Ashlyn and leave the rest of you."

"Go ahead," Nikki said.

"I should," the young man said petulantly.

"She didn't mean anything," Ashlyn said soothingly, stroking the young man's arm.

Shrugging off her attentions, he went to Kimberly, and stopped before her. "I've never seen *you* before."

"Kimberly Kilpatrick," Ashlyn said, "this is my boyfriend, Gregory Rose."

He looked down at her and sneered. " 'The vanity of others offends our taste only when it offends *our* vanity.' "

Kimberly recoiled as if she had been struck. She hadn't been entirely certain this guy could form com-

41

plete sentences, let alone deliver a quote like that.

"I guess you've never read Nietzsche," he said. "I suppose you've also made some snap judgment about me 'cause of the way I dress, the way I talk."

Kimberly swallowed and said nothing.

"I'm the lead singer for the Berserkers," he went on. "I write the lyrics, too. Ashlyn saw me on stage and came back to see me one night. That's how we got started."

"The Berserkers," Kimberly said, trying to place the name.

"They're a bar band right now. They tour the state and even play gigs in the city once in a while," Ashlyn said with a touch of pride.

" 'The great epochs of our life come when we gain the courage to rechristen our evil as what is best in us.' " His smile was cold and terrible. "That means that sometimes it's good to be bad. Nietzsche was a wise man. You want to be bad, don't you? That's why you're here."

Kimberly cleared her throat and was about to speak when Nikki interrupted.

"Nietzsche was a sexist piglet. He also said that 'when a woman has scholarly inclinations there is usually something wrong with her sexually.' I've been reading up on your hero, Greg."

He shrugged, then spun suddenly and struck Kimberly in the mouth. Her jaw rattled and she issued a quick cry of surprise. Then she was falling to her knees. Nikki ran forward and grabbed her.

"Gregory!" Ashlyn shouted as she reached for him. He raised his clenched fist in her direction and she froze.

" 'One has to repay good and ill—but why precisely to the person who has done us good or ill?' " Gregory said, quoting more of Nietzsche's philosophy. "In other words, paybacks are hell."

"Get out of here," Ashlyn snarled.

Kimberly caught Ashlyn's eye and shook her head

42

slightly. She struggled to restrain her tears. Her recent experiences with Sharon had strengthened her and she wanted Ashlyn to know she would not collapse emotionally under Gregory's assault.

"I thought you needed a ride," Gregory said.

"Go," Tanya said.

Shaking his head, Gregory took a small package from his jacket pocket. It looked like a case for a ring. "This *was* your anniversary gift," he said, then hurled the case deep into the thicket.

Ashlyn's body tightened. Kimberly thought she seemed angry with herself for the slight movement of her legs in the direction of the discarded present.

Rose walked back to his truck and opened the driver's side door. Before he got in, he said, " 'Whatever is done from love always occurs beyond good and evil.' Remember that, Ashlyn. Happy anniversary!"

He climbed behind the wheel and took off. His black truck growled as it tore past them and went down the winding road, disappearing from view within seconds.

"Yeah, happy anniversary, you creep," Ashlyn whispered. "Happy anniversary."

Seven

"So now what do we do?" Tanya asked. She stood at the side of the road, hugging herself. A slight chill had risen.

"We've got to get Kimberly back to Cooper," Ashlyn said. "I don't know how bad he hurt her. He could have broken her jaw, the jerk."

Kimberly's mind was swimming. She held her hands to her face, refusing to allow Ashlyn or Nikki to pry them away. A part of her simply could not accept what had happened to her. The meeting with Gregory Rose had been violent and brief—so brief it made Kimberly wonder if it had been nothing more than another terrible nightmare. But the throbbing pain in her face told her differently.

"You're going to be all right," Ashlyn said softly. "Let me see."

Reluctantly, Kimberly dropped her hands. She had been afraid that her jaw would fall off the moment she stopped holding it. Now, opening and closing her mouth, working her jaw from side to side, Kimberly felt a flood of relief.

"You're going to have a bruise, but I don't think it'll be any worse than that," Ashlyn said, her relief mirroring Kimberly's.

"I don't want to go back," Kimberly said, finally risking speech. She expected her words to sound much more slurred than they actually did.

"You've got to get ice on that," Ashlyn said. "It must hurt like a mother."

44

"It does," Kimberly said. "But I don't care. I don't want to go back."

Kimberly watched as Ashlyn stared into her eyes. She knew what the other girl was seeing—a resolve that would not be argued with. Her aunt had called her the most stubborn, belligerent kid she had ever known. That was unfair, of course. Kimberly rarely spoke back. Nevertheless, as far as her aunt was concerned, even holding an independent opinion was overstepping the boundaries. Her aunt had come to know the look Kimberly wore now, and understood how pointless it was to argue with her. Ashlyn apparently sensed the exact same thing because she hung her head and sighed.

"What, we're gonna walk into town?" Nikki asked sarcastically.

As if in response, a pair of headlights suddenly pierced the darkness. Kimberly's inner fires flickered and died immediately. She was terrified that Rose had come back. Then she heard the music coming from the car's open windows. It sounded like an organ riff from "Phantom of the Opera."

A man's voice, deep and somewhat overdramatic, spoke to them from the approaching vehicle. *"Escape! From now, from here, from yourself. Columbia invites you to voyage into the realms of the imagination. Each week we present adventures of men and women who escape into the misty lands between the credible and the incredible."*

The words were followed by another burst of organ music. Kimberly recognized it as some kind of old time radio show. "We better get away from here," she said, attempting to keep the fear she felt out of her voice. The others were unmoving as the headlights of the approaching car washed over them and the vehicle ground to a halt on the road's narrow shoulder. It was a red Tempo with a single occupant. Kimberly had seen enough "true crime" TV movies to realize they had all the elements in place for a juicy entry in the pantheon of tasteless recreations: Four young girls who had

45

skipped out of their boarding school and wouldn't be missed until morning. Some old man — he must be old, listening to that radio stuff — who might seem friendly at first, until he broke out the handcuffs, or a gun. She shuddered, realizing that even if she turned out to be the only one with enough sense to turn and run back into the woods, she did not know the way back to the school from here.

The driver's side door opened and a figure emerged in silhouette. He came around the side of the car and the headlights revealed him to be a tall, trim young man wearing a gray tee-shirt, a leather jacket, blue jeans, and Nikes. Around his neck was a small black trinket. Kimberly thought it might have been a cross, but as the boy came closer, she saw that it was a strange, unfamiliar symbol, with a large, hexagonal crown and a dagger-like lower half.

Wonderful, she thought. I can see the headlines now. Cultists kidnap, torture, and slay innocent teens. We'll probaby make "A Current Affair" *and* "Hard Copy."

Then she looked up at his face, and her fears were washed away by what she saw in his soft brown eyes. They were gentle and more than a little sad. She could not identify his nationality. He might have been Italian, possibly Jewish. His hair was dark, rich, and full, immaculately groomed, cut short in the back. The boy's jaw was slightly rounded, but very strong. He was broad-shouldered, with cheekbones that stopped just short of being chiseled and a large nose that was the only less-than perfect element in his beautiful face. The nose made him seem flawed, human, and vulnerable.

He went directly to the kneeling Kimberly and crouched before her. "Are you all right?"

Her heart skipped a beat. She had read that line in books a thousand times and until that moment, had had no idea what it meant. She did not try to stand, fearing that she would also learn what "watery legs" meant.

The boy's voice was lightly accented — a Brooklyn

46

transplant, perhaps — and entirely deep, smooth.

"Beauty and the Beast," she thought. He sounds a little like the Beast in his gentle moments.

"Are you all right?" he asked again with concern.

"I'm okay," she said.

"You must be freezing," he asked.

"No," she whispered, feeling the flare of her inner fires, which were once again burning brightly.

"You ladies need a ride somewhere?" He had mentioned the other girls, but his gaze had never wavered from Kimberly. Likewise, she could not keep herself from staring into his perfect brown eyes.

"Yeah," Kimberly said, finally tearing her eyes away from this boy's handsome face and looking to Ashlyn. "What do you think?"

"I don't know. Can all five of us fit in your car?"

"Sure," he said. "If you give me a minute to haul some of my junk out and stuff it in the trunk."

Kimberly realized that he preferred listening to her and not the others. "Yeah, that's fine."

Smiling warmly, the boy rose and walked back to his car. He opened the trunk and went around to the back.

"I don't know how smart this is," Kimberly admitted now that he was out of ear-shot.

Nikki frowned. "I know exactly how smart this *isn't*."

Ashlyn opened her bag and withdrew a small black cylinder. "Mace. We'll be okay." Nikki's frown did not disappear. "Look, we all need a night out. And as long as Kimberly's OK, I'm not going to let Greg spoil it for us. If you want to go back and let him win, that's up to you."

"All right," Nikki said. "We go."

Kimberly nodded. The pain in her jaw was beginning to worsen. The boy finished at the car and motioned for the girls to come over.

"You notice he didn't even ask what we were doing out here?" Tanya said. "And he didn't ask how you got hurt? Isn't that the first thing you would have thought to ask?"

"I dunno," Kimberly said. "Maybe."

"It just makes me worry, that's all."

"Easy enough to fix that," Ashlyn said as she reached the boy first and questioned him.

"Well, it's none of my business," he said. "I figured you'd get around to telling me sooner or later. Or not. The only thing that's important is getting you girls where you need to go so you can get some help."

Ashlyn looked at Tanya. "Good enough for me."

"Me, too," Kimberly said, then held her hand out and introduced herself.

He took her hand. "Joel Griffiths. 'Griff' is fine. That's what everyone calls me."

"You don't like 'Joel'?" Kimberly asked, flushed at the touch of his hand. She had no idea what love at first sight was all about, but she certainly felt *something* for this boy. Something she had never felt before in her life.

"I like it okay. Griff is just what everyone calls me. Especially my friends."

Kimberly smiled, despite the brief flare of pain it caused. "All right," she said softly. "Griff."

Eight

"Well, if you're not going to be nosy, I am," Kimberly said. She sat in the driver's side bucket seat, next to Griff. Ashlyn, Nikki, and Tanya were squashed together in the back. They had asked Griff to take them into town and were nearly there. "How come you're out driving so late?"

"I wanted to get out of the house. My mom was driving me crazy," he said. "I'm starting to look at stuff on different colleges and she's taken it up like it's a holy crusade or something. Y'know, it was fun before, when I was doing it for myself, but it's not so much fun getting it crammed down your throat. She means well, but it still drives me crazy."

"What does your dad think about that?"

"He died a few years back."

"I'm sorry."

"I'm not."

Kimberly looked over at him in shock.

"I know the way that sounds, but he was a drunk and he used to hit my mom. They were separated. One day we just got this phone call. I was sure he had finally had a car accident while he was plastered, and I was sure he would have taken some innocent people with him. But it was an aneurism. A vessel in his brain burst and he was gone."

"And you were okay with that?" Kimberly asked, dimly aware that three other people sat in the backseat of the car.

"I must sound pretty cold," he said. "I guess that makes me a terrible person, huh?"

49

"No," Kimberly said. She barely knew him, but she was certain of that much. "You are *not* a terrible person."

"I never cried, never felt anything but relief. The nightmare was over. No more screaming phone calls ruining holidays. No more having to get the police to drag him out of the house. No more having to get our support money every other week at his damned bars so he could show off to his drunk friends that he had a good son. No more. I was just glad it was over."

Kimberly was overwhelmed. This was an incredibly personal disclosure for anyone to make—particularly under these circumstances—to a girl he barely knew.

"I guess I'm too hard on my mom, sometimes. I don't want to give her any more grief. She's had enough."

"My parents died when I was young," Kimberly said. "I miss them a lot."

"I'm sorry."

A rustling came from the backseat, startling Kimberly.

"My mom is a vulture," Tanya said in her hazy voice. "She just circles and circles, waiting for an opening. The second you show any sign of weakness—bam! She goes for you. So you have to stay on guard all the time. You can never just relax as long as you're in the house with her. That's why I made up every excuse I could to get away from there. When I got the chance to come to Cooper, I jumped at it. *Anything* to get away from her. Now things are different. Now that I'm a Predator, *everything's* different."

"Go into that strip mall, over there on the right," Ashlyn said suddenly. Griff did as she asked, taking them to a parking space directly before a twenty-four hour pharmacy. He had correctly assumed they were stopping to get something for Kimberly's bruise.

"I've got money. I'll go," Ashlyn said. She got out of the car and went inside.

Nikki kicked at the back of Griff's seat. "So, do you

50

tell your life story to every carload of strange girls you pick up, or are we something special?"

He wasn't telling it to you, he was telling it to *me*, Kimberly thought heatedly.

"I don't know. I just felt like talking."

"What about these tapes you have," Kimberly said, attempting to change the subject and help Griff dodge any further embarrassing questions. She dug through his collection of cassettes which rested in the hollow between their seats. Most of them were recordings of that old radio show, "The Shadow" with Orson Welles. " 'The Whistler,' 'X-Minus One,' 'I Love a Mystery,' 'Escape.' You're really into this."

"Yeah, I dunno. They're just cool. A lot of them have really good stories. Especially 'Escape.' "

The answer was not what Kimberly wanted to hear. She imagined that if Nikki had kept her mouth shut, Griff would have told her how he had discovered these old shows, and what he really got out of them. His reticence was clearly a result of Nikki shooting off her mouth, and that angered her.

"My aunt and uncle ignored me, so I read a lot," Kimberly said, attempting to repair the sudden breach.

"Your aunt and uncle?"

Kimberly briefly told him the story of her parents' death. If she had been alone with Griff, she might have told him that it had been her fault.

Ashlyn returned with a bag she handed to Kimberly. Kimberly drew out a package of ice, a Coke, and a bottle of Advil. She popped open the soda, took three caplets, and downed them immediately. The plastic bag of ice was freezing cold to the touch. She was about to set it on her jaw when Griff asked her to wait. He stepped out of the car and took off his jacket. Then he removed the small necklace and stripped off his shirt. Kimberly's cheeks flushed in embarrassment at the sight of his muscular and perfectly defined body.

Ashlyn and Nikki howled and whistled, causing

Griff to frown good-naturedly as he handed Kimberly the tee-shirt and told her to wrap the ice in it. Then he put on the necklace, slipped his jacket over his bare flesh, and zipped it up. Ashlyn and Nikki made sounds of disappointment. Tanya did not even seem to notice.

"Ashlyn," Tanya said in her dreamy voice, "did you know that Kimberly's parents were killed in an accident? You two have a lot in common."

Ashlyn's features hardened. "I told you that I don't want to talk about that. Or have you forgotten?"

"I want to go to the Night Owl," Nikki said quickly, probably, Kimberly thought, to curtail a possible blow-up between Ashlyn and Tanya. She punched the back of Griff's seat. "You know where that is?"

Griff looked at Kimberly in confusion. Evidently, he had expected to take the girls home. She nodded, though she had no idea what the "Night Owl" was. As they were about to pull out of the parking lot, a black pick-up cut them off. Griff slammed on the brakes to avoid a collision. The pick-up did not even slow.

"Complete A-hole," Griff said, his chest heaving. "I swear to God." He looked at Kimberly. "You okay?"

She nodded, shaken. She had seen the driver of the pick-up, which was now filled with a half-dozen screaming males. It had been Gregory Rose, the monster who had struck her. A part of her wanted to tell Griff what had happened earlier, and get him to go after Rose. But Ashlyn's boyfriend was not alone, and she didn't want Griff to get hurt.

"I'm fine," Kimberly said. "Really."

Nine

They went to the Night Owl Club, heading in the same general direction from which they had come, but taking a different road, one filled with hair-pin turns and covered by canopies of narrow old trees that seemed to have withered and turned black over the centuries.

Along the drive, there was little conversation. Kimberly was tempted to ask Griff to put on one of his tapes, but Nikki leaned forward from her spot in the middle of the backseat and turned on the radio, blasting them with rock music. When Tanya protested, Nikki reached forward once more, turning the radio off.

Finally, Griff pulled into a parking lot in which dozens of cars were gathered. Kimberly scanned the lot and was relieved to note the absence of Gregory Rose's black pick-up. She turned her attention to the large, two-story brick building looming just ahead. It looked almost as menacing to Kimberly as the reconverted hotel that housed the Cooper Riding Academy. Suddenly, she registered music coming from inside.

"The Night Owl is a *club?*" Kimberly said as the five got out of the car. "I've never heard of this place."

"This place used to be an orphanage," Griff said. "The owners mistreated the kids. They took their food money and let the kids starve. If any of them complained, they were beaten. Couple hundred kids died there before it was all over. Burned to death in a fire, I think. A lot of weird things happen here. Some kids call it the Night*mare* Club."

"What a nice little spot for a nightclub," Kimberly said with an involuntary shudder.

"A *kid's* club."

"Wonderful. I'd like to meet the creeps who thought that was funny."

"You probably will. The owner and his daughter are always there."

"Well, at least we don't have to worry about being carded."

"Nope."

"How do you know so much about this place?"

"There was a big controversy in the local papers. A lot of editorials going back and forth about it. I've been involved in—"

Tanya suddenly brushed past Kimberly and walked to the club's front door over which hung a blue light. When Tanya opened the door and stepped inside, an explosion of sound—the monotonous beat of industrial music—rushed out to greet the others. They followed Tanya inside.

The interior of the club was far different from what Kimberly had expected, considering the oppressive outside of the building. The club's main room held not only the dance floor—complete with a shining, faceted silver ball hanging from the rafters—but also a game room, snack bar, and dozens of booths. The group went to one of the booths and sat down. The red leather cushions on the seats were very warm. The only light came from candles housed in colored glass bowls on the tables.

"Never thought I'd see the day when Nine Inch Nails got a display in the window at Camelot's," Nikki said. "Progressive is getting mainstreamed."

Kimberly nodded, though she had no idea who Nine Inch Nails were. The last time she had been to any music store was six months earlier, and Cooper only allowed the students to access preselected channels on the television in the "game room." Arts and Entertainment was in, MTV was out.

An attractive young blond waitress appeared, carrying an order pad. Ashlyn ordered drinks for everyone. Smiling, the blond woman walked away. Ashlyn went off to dance with Tanya. Nikki sat at the table with Kimberly and Griff for a few moments, then must have realized the extent to which her presence was unwelcome and was decent enough to leave them alone. Nikki might *seem* mean-spirted at times, Kimberly realized, but she was usually just looking for attention.

When they were alone, Griff said, "Rose better not let me anywhere near him for a while."

Kimberly, still holding the ice to her jaw, was stunned. "You know that guy?"

"Sure. He was a senior last year. I can't believe the way he came at us. If I had been a little slower, he would have plowed into your side of the car. Drunk as a skunk, just like my dad."

Kimberly knew she had been right not to tell Griff about Rose striking her. His knowing would only cause him trouble.

"You can ask *me* questions, if you want," Kimberly said. "It's okay."

He nodded. "What happened to you? Your mouth?"

His question startled her. It was like he'd been reading her mind.

"I tripped and fell in the woods," she said quickly.

"Where do you go to school?"

"Cooper Riding Academy," she said, relieved to be able to answer that one honestly. "We snuck out tonight."

He nodded. "When do you have to be back?"

"I guess before six. In the morning, that is."

"You don't want to get any sleep?"

"I don't really feel tired." That was true. Despite all she had been through that night, or, perhaps, because of it, Kimberly was wired.

"Do you want to dance?" Griff asked.

Kimberly shrugged. "I'm not very good," she admitted.

"Neither am I. But look at our competition."

Kimberly laughed realizing that only a few couples on the dance floor had any coordination at all. "I guess you're right. But this isn't really the kind of music I like dancing to."

"What *do* you like?"

"Well, I don't know. Slower songs, mostly."

"That's fine." Griff got up and went to the jukebox. When he returned a few moments later he said, "Our songs will be up in a few minutes. Your friends seem to be having a good time."

Kimberly turned her attention to the dance floor. All three of the Predators were dancing together, attracting the attention of every boy in the club. They seemed to love being the center of attention. They seemed to revel in the power it gave them.

The deafening sounds of industrial pop trailed away, replaced by a Vanessa Williams ballad. Griff held out his hand and Kimberly took it. He led her to the dance floor. She was terrified that she would disappoint him, but after a few moments, she relaxed. Griff was a wonderful dancer. And in his arms, so was she. They danced through four songs in a row, Kimberly's head firmly pressed against his chest.

As the fourth song ended, Kimberly felt the pain in her jaw returning. She turned from him quickly, so that he could not see her expression.

"I'll be right back, okay?" Kimberly said.

"Yeah," Griff said. His deep brown eyes were troubled. She knew he was wondering if he had done something wrong. Surprising herself once again, Kimberly leaned up and kissed his cheek. The apprehension vanished from his eyes.

Kimberly stayed in the bathroom, applying ice cold water to the side of her face for five minutes, until the pain had ebbed. She hated the idea of being away from Griff. What if he left without her? What if Nikki played one of her jokes and told him Kimberly was mad at him and didn't want to see him any more?

She was being paranoid. Why should Griff matter so much to her, she wondered. She barely knew him.

That's not true. You know him. You've been waiting for him all your life.

Kimberly left the rest room and was stunned to see Gregory Rose and Griff in a standoff, several of Rose's friends surrounding them on the dance floor.

Ten

Kimberly didn't know what to do. A part of her wanted to run and hide. Ignoring that impulse, she stepped closer to the scene of the conflict. Before she was noticed by either Griff or Gregory Rose, a hawk-nosed man burst through the circle of spectators and stepped between the two.

"Rose, you little piece of rat-snot, I thought I told you that you and your friends weren't welcome here," the older man said fiercely. "Now get out!"

"Why should we?" Rose asked. "What're you gonna do, Demos, call the police?"

For the briefest instant, the older man's eyes seemed to blaze. He drew his withered lips back in a feral grin. "What, and spoil all *my* fun?"

Rose shuddered. "Cold in here," he said, attempting to deny the fear that had suddenly risen in him. He motioned for his friends to follow him as he turned and walked toward the door.

"This isn't over," Griff said to Rose's departing form.

" 'One is best punished for one's virtues,' " Rose replied. Then he and his friends left the club.

Kimberly went to Griff's side. "What happened?"

"What always happens when you put Gregory Rose and me in the same room. We've always been like this. Hate at first sight."

The white-haired man who had come between Griff and Rose approached. He was frowning, and from the lines in his face, that seemed to be the man's most comfortable expression. To Kimberly, his high forehead,

58

puff of pure white hair, and hooked nose made him look like a professor from an old "Twilight Zone," but the sharpness she saw in his eyes and the harshness of his voice marked him as anything but kindly.

"My name's Jake Demos," he said, addressing Griff. "I own this place. I don't want trouble. Tell your friends—"

"They're not my friends."

"You don't know much, do you, boy?" Demos snarled. "I'm aware of that. I'm also aware that you're going to tangle with them again. Fine. Maybe the bunch of you will just put each other in the hospital. At least that would save me the bother of deciding what to do if I see any of you again."

"Griff didn't start this," Kimberly said.

"Actually, I did," Griff said. "Not in the first place. But I did, tonight."

"That's why I'm talking to you, boy," Demos continued. "I'm no stranger to trouble. I've seen more than you would ever think possible. Now I want quiet." Demos punctuated each word with a little poke to Griff's chest. *"Peace and quiet.* You understand?"

"You bet."

"I told Rose and his band I didn't want them playing here on weekends. They stink. But they keep showing up, bringing down the property values, if you know what I mean. I want them out of my hair. What's left of it."

"I'll see what I can do."

"You do that."

"I will."

With a sharp nod, Demos stalked off. Before Griff could say anything further, Ashlyn appeared.

"All done," she said.

"Maybe we should go," Griff said.

"Rose might be hanging around the parking lot waiting for us," Kimberly said, looking desperately for any excuse to dance one more dance in Griff's arms. "I'd feel better if we waited it out for a little bit."

59

"Sure," Griff said. "If that's okay with the rest of you girls."

Ashlyn, Nikki, and Tanya gave their assent, and the next hour passed quickly for Kimberly. She and Griff danced to another half a dozen songs. Then they went through the arched doorway leading to the game room. Besides video games, there were pool, air hockey, and fooz ball tables.

"I've never actually played pool before," Kimberly said. It wasn't true. Her uncle had a pool table in the basement. Kimberly had always been very strict with herself about lying. But tonight, she couldn't help herself. A few white lies wouldn't hurt anyone, she reasoned. Griff didn't need to know that Rose had hit her—or that she was a great pool player.

Kimberly allowed Griff to stand behind her, helping to position her arms and legs. The feel of his body near hers was worth paying any price, including the sacrifice of one of her principles.

While they played two games—games Kimberly allowed Griff to win—Griff told Kimberly about how he'd come to love the old radio shows. He'd begun to listen to radio plays when he was very young. When his parents were arguing in the other room, Griff would turn the radio on to drown out the hateful sounds. At some point one station began a revival of old time radio shows and Griff became hooked. The shows transported him from his nightmarish, waking reality. They allowed him to be an active partner in creating another, better reality, and helped him to find a sanctuary from the brutality of his early life. Kimberly thought she understood Griff's attachment to the shows, his need to keep listening to them even after his father's death.

Suddenly, Ashlyn appeared and announced that they had to get back to the school. Griff offered to drive them, and Ashlyn accepted.

When they reached the spot in the woods where Griff had first picked them up, he pulled his car off onto the narrow shoulder. Ashlyn, Nikki, and Tanya got out of the car and started back in the direction of the boarding school. Kimberly called to them to wait, but they did not slow down.

Realizing their goodbye had to be brief, dying to kiss Griff and knowing that it was too soon, Kimberly got out of the car and leaned in through the open window.

"When can I see you again?" he asked.

Thank God, she thought. He wanted to see her, too. She had to think quickly. Ashlyn and the others were almost out of view. "I have a weekend pass. I'll be home all weekend."

"I don't know where that is," he said.

There was no time to tell him. Even if she gave him her phone number, he might lose it. Worse, her aunt and uncle might not approve of her getting calls from "strange" boys—any boys, for that matter. They might intercept the call, or simply not allow her to see him.

"The club," she said quickly. "Friday night at seven. We'll meet there."

His answering smile took her breath away. That was another of those phrases she had always seen in books and never understood. Until now.

"Kimberly!" a faint voice called. Ashlyn. She turned and could no longer see her friends.

"You better get going," Griff said.

She nodded, worried that she would not be able to get back into school on her own, and annoyed that her friends were not giving her more time with Griff. Of course, they *had* given her that extra hour at the club.

"Friday," she said, picking up the icepack from the carseat. It was still wrapped in his moist tee-shirt.

"You know it."

She hurried from the car, stealing a backward glance as she heard him pull away. Then she plunged into the woods.

Eleven

The chill she had shut out earlier came now, swirling around her and clutching at her like a cape buffeted by a monstrous wind. Even thoughts of Griff could not drive out the cold that was seeping into her heart. Ashlyn had left her behind. She had called her friend's name, but received no reply.

Don't panic, she thought. There's bound to be a way out of this.

She didn't know the woods at all. Her uncle had only moved them to Cooper Hollow six months ago, and she had never explored them. Even if she had, it was dark, and she had almost no innate sense of direction.

Try to remember how you got here, she urged herself.

Her efforts failed her. She wandered deeper into the woods, occasionally hearing the scurrying sounds of small animals, or the rustling of leaves high above. Her own footsteps were incredibly loud, almost as loud as her thundering heart. She tried to move slowly, worried that she would trip and knock herself unconscious. All she needed was to wake up in the woods the next morning when she should have been in bed, at Cooper. If she wasn't thrown out, she would at least be punished and humiliated.

Suddenly, she thought of the Sunday afternoons when her uncle had his partners over. They had been frat buddies back in college and after graduation they had opened a law firm together. When they reminisced, which was often, they turned into little boys talking about the pranks they played and the humiliating rites of initiation they had inflicted on their frat pledges.

Was this some part of her Initiation into the Predators?

God, she was terrified. She hated being lost. The thought of spending the night in the woods made her want to cry like a child, and she hated herself for that weakness. Suddenly, she heard a sound. A branch being shoved out of the way. Something heavy striking the earth with a dull thud.

Someone was close. The girls had not abandoned her, they were playing. Trying to spook her.

Fine, they were succeeding.

The sound came again. This time she identified the direction from which it had come. Behind her. She turned and saw something pale disappear behind a tree.

Funny. Hilarious. Just great, girls. I really appreciate it. Now cut the crap and let's get out of here, she thought.

The words skated across the surface of her mind, but she didn't have the courage to voice them. She tried to assimilate the image her eyes had registered. She was certain that whatever she had seen had glistened, that it was dripping wet, but that made no sense at all.

Then she recalled that there was a lake nearby. Ashlyn and her pals were working overtime to tax her nerves. Terrific. As if she hadn't been through enough during the last few days.

The rustling came again, and with it a sound all too familiar to her: the clomping of hooves.

The paths were too narrow. How could a horse get out here in the first place? They didn't exactly run wild in Cooper Hollow. It must have come from the school, and getting out with a horse would be a much more difficult task than what they had achieved this night. Impossible, even.

The sound came again, accompanied by the soft chuffing of a mount expelling a breath. Kimberly was not afraid of the horse. She had been around horses long enough to feel comfortable with them.

The animal broke into a gallop. Kimberly heard twigs break, roots and hard earth crunch underfoot, branches being swept out of the way. She was not going to run. A horse could not get to her where she stood. The path was too narrow. It would knock itself out before it reached her.

Again, the shuffling. She looked ahead and saw a bright, luminescent figure. An auburn-haired girl, soaking wet.

Ashlyn.

Behind her, the sounds magnified and the ground seemed to shake. She spun and nearly screamed as she saw Ashlyn standing before her, reaching for her, looking the same as before. She was not wet in the least. Nikki and Tanya crowded behind her. They were also dry. Kimberly turned back to the shimmering girl, but no one was there.

"Where the hell were you?" Ashlyn said, her eyes wide with concern, her chest heaving. "I thought you were right behind us. We almost got lost trying to find you. Didn't you hear us calling your name?"

"Only once, when I was still at the car."

Ashlyn let out a shuddering breath. "At least you're okay. That's all that matters. Let's get back to Cooper. You're going to be wiped out in the morning."

Kimberly thought briefly about telling her friends what she had seen and then decided against it. If they had heard what she had heard, seen what she had seen, they would have mentioned something, right?

So maybe she was hallucinating. Maybe she was going crazy. Or maybe someone was trying to make her *think* she was insane. Who would want to do such a thing?

Sharon.

It made no sense, of course. Kimberly tried to reason how Sharon could have pulled off the stunt that had just taken place in the woods. Her efforts failed. Still, her anger did not subside.

Gregory Rose wasn't the only person alive to ever have read the philosopher Nietzsche. Kimberly's uncle had one of his books and she'd flipped through it once or twice. A quote now came to her: "In revenge and in love woman is more barbarous than man."

Twelve

The next day, Kimberly went to the infirmary and had the bruise on her jaw looked at. She claimed that she had fallen out of bed and her story was believed. The nurse gave her painkillers and told her to be more careful. None of the other students commented on the bruise. They took one look at Kimberly's constant companion, Ashlyn, and knew they didn't dare open their mouths.

On the way to class, Ashlyn asked Kimberly if she was clear for the weekend.

Kimberly nodded. "I don't think my uncle was thrilled but I don't care much about that. He won't have to see me that often. I want to spend every minute I can with Griff."

"You're pretty sure about this thing you've got with him?"

Kimberly suddenly felt lightheaded at the thought of going out with him Friday night.

"Don't answer that," Ashlyn said, a slight smile on her lips. "I can see it in your eyes."

"The only thing I'm worried about is your boyfriend."

"Ex-boyfriend."

"What *is* it between them?" Kimberly asked, "Did Gregory ever mention Griff?"

"Never. But then, he didn't talk much. Not unless he wanted something or wanted to quote from one of his books. I must have been crazy for hanging around with him for so long." Ashlyn bit her lip and nodded at the bruise on Kimberly's face. "Does it still hurt?"

"Not too bad. Nurse Jemison gave me something for the pain."

Ashlyn nodded. "Yeah. I was worried that the pain had kept you awake."

"No, not at all," Kimberly said, smiling reassuringly.

Ashlyn looked at her watch. "Good. Look, we both better get to class."

Kimberly nodded and they went in separate directions. As she entered her classroom and took her seat, Kimberly thought of her dream, the real reason she'd had a good night's rest. The gray horse had visited her again last night. She had climbed upon the animal and had been taken on a wondrous ride through a magical woods. Occasionally, they encountered children playing in the woods, or on the shore of the lake outside the woods. Kimberly approached the children, helped them to get astride the animal, then howled with delight as the gray horse carried the laughing children away.

At times during the dream she seemed aware of the similarity between the fantasy woods and those outside the school. It wasn't significant, of course. All woods looked alike.

Besides, why should she think too much about her dreams, when her waking life was better than it had ever been?

And that's what it must have been, the other night, she thought. The figure she saw, the noises she heard. She had been daydreaming; her imagination had gotten the better of her. That was all.

With a lightness of heart she generally never felt except when riding, Kimberly entered the classroom and began the long wait until her second date with Griff.

Her happiness was short-lived. Class began and the results of last week's test were distributed. Kimberly had scored a solid "D." A few days ago she had been dying to be sent away from Cooper. Now she had friends, status, and even an element of control over her own life — something she had never had before. Her

66

heart began to race. Somehow, she had to do better. She would spend her every free moment studying if she needed to. Anything so that she would not have to give up what she had so recently attained.

Kimberly's teacher called for everyone's attention and delivered the opening speech in a long monologue. A few moments later, Kimberly's eyes drifted back to the paper before her.

The grade was a "B," not a "D" as she had first believed. It was impossible. She was *certain* that the lower grade had been correct, but when she examined the test once again, the better mark was indisputable, written there in ink.

Don't argue with it, a voice deep within whispered. *Don't think about it too much. This is what you wanted. This is what you needed. Take it.*

Smiling, Kimberly looked up from the paper, feeling a degree of relief she hadn't believed possible.

Class dragged on and Kimberly could think of nothing but Griff. She knew that her teacher was discussing semester finals, outlining the areas on which the test would concentrate, but she found that she wasn't worried about the test. She would do all right, she thought. There was no reason to be concerned.

After class, Kimberly found herself daydreaming in the hall. Suddenly, she heard the bell go off. Starting, she looked at her watch—and then recalled that she had this period free.

She wandered outside and came to the Mansfield dorms, in which Sharon's room was located. She walked into the building without being seen and went to the third floor, pausing at the head of the stairs to note that the corridor was empty. Without looking back, she went directly to Sharon's room and tried the door.

Locked. She turned away, thought better of it, and tried the door again. This time, it gave. Though it *had* been locked, it mustn't have been closed properly. She went inside and shut the door behind her.

67

The room was threadbare. Anything that would have made it more personal had been removed or hidden away. Sharon knew that her room wasn't safe, just as Kimberly's had not been.

That was all right. Kimberly just wanted to leave a message. She dug into her pockets and removed a small lipstick that Ashlyn had given her. Ashlyn had spent time teaching Kimberly the best way to apply makeup, something her aunt had never bothered to show her. Wearing makeup on the school grounds was frowned upon, but the girls were free to do as they liked in the confines of their rooms.

Kimberly wrote a single word over and over, covering the mirror and each of the walls. She ran from surface to surface, giggling hysterically as she scribbled the word, filling up the space that had been stark white only moments ago.

Reject! she wrote. She wanted to scrawl it once for every time she had heard the word from Sharon's lips, for every time one of Sharon's friends had said it to her. To do so, she would have run out of lipstick and wall space.

Out of breath from all the running around, Kimberly left Sharon's room, slamming the door shut. She took three steps and heard someone clearing their throat behind her. Panic seized Kimberly until she turned and saw the face of a short, fat, red-head.

Thelma Hopkins. The girl who was supposed to have endured the year-long "Rite of Passage." Kimberly would have taken her place, if not for Ashlyn. Suddenly, Kimberly wondered if Sharon had been taking out her frustration on this girl. It made sense, after all. No one was going to defend Thelma Hopkins, least of all Thelma herself.

The brief surge of pity Kimberly felt was replaced by anger as the memory of Thelma's presence during her ordeal came back to her. Thelma had been willing, reluctantly or not, to participate in Kimberly's hazing to avoid enduring the ritual herself. That fact erased all good will Kimberly might have held for the girl.

But you felt relieved when you thought it had been Thelma instead of you, the nagging voice in Kimberly's head reminded her. *If the situations were reversed, you might have done the same, just stood by and watched. Doesn't that make a difference?*

I wouldn't have done that, Kimberly thought fiercely. So, no, it's *not* the same. It's not the same at all.

"You know who I am, right?" Kimberly said sharply.

The girl nodded. "Yes, Ms. Kilpatrick."

Kimberly could not restrain a smile. *Ms. Kilpatrick.* She loved it. "And, if anyone asks, you haven't seen me here today. That's right, isn't it?"

Thelma swallowed hard. "Yeah, that's right."

"Because if you say anything—"

The red-head's eyes flashed open wide. "I won't, I promise!"

Kimberly was surprised to find how much she enjoyed the look of fear in Thelma's eyes. She had *power* over this girl. Complete power. "See that you don't. I'm not someone you want to mess with."

"I know that. Yes, Ms. Kilpatrick. I understand. You don't have to worry about me."

Kimberly turned and walked away slowly, fighting her impulses to run and laugh and scream with delight.

Thirteen

On Friday night, Kimberly found Griff waiting at the same booth they had chosen the last time they were in the club. They were both very nervous at first, as if they weren't quite sure that what passed between them the other night had been real. After a half hour of talking about life in Cooper Hollow, both relaxed and accepted that they had not deluded themselves. Something very special was happening between them.

Suddenly, Kimberly realized that Griff's necklace was missing. She had wanted to ask him about the oddly designed item the other night and had never gotten around to it.

"You're not wearing your chain," she said. Griff shifted uncomfortably in his chair and Kimberly immediately kicked herself for making her words sound like a criticism.

"I lost it," he said, his expression darkening. "I really don't know how. It was pretty special to me."

"I'm sorry," Kimberly said, suddenly concerned by the swell of anger she sensed in him. "We don't have to—"

"No, I *want* to talk about it," he said. "My parents had three kids, but I was, y'know, the baby of the family. My older brother and sister left home when I was a kid. Couldn't stand being around my father. I can't blame them. My sister gave me the pendant when I was a kid. The next weekend she got killed in an accident at her college. A bus overturned. So I kept the necklace. Never took it off.

"The only thing I can think of is that I lost it during

track. The clasp must have come open somehow. They take us outside the school grounds to run for a couple of miles. It must have fallen off along the route. I've been over that stretch a dozen times, but I haven't been able to find it."

"I'm sorry." Kimberly's fingers grazed his hand. "What about your brother? Do you ever see him?"

"No. He and a buddy of his have an import/export business in China. Once in a while we get a Christmas card."

Hesitantly, Kimberly led into the full story of how her real parents were killed the day before her ninth birthday and of how it had been her fault.

"You can't blame yourself," Griff said compassionately when she had finished. "I'm sure if your real parents were standing here right now, they'd tell you how glad they were that you're okay, that you didn't die with them. I'm sure they loved you very much and would have only wanted what was best for you."

You're what's best for me, Kimberly thought, her heart expanding. Determined to restore the upbeat mood, Kimberly said, "I have an idea: You can give me another lesson at pool. That is, if you think you're up for it."

Griff smiled. "Oh, I'm up to it, all right."

This time, Kimberly did not bother to hide her skill at the game. She played hard and won.

"You got better," Griff said in surprise.

"I whipped your *butt,*" she said with a laugh.

"Yeah, okay, you did."

Kimberly's smile faltered. She wondered if she made a mistake. This boy-girl thing was hard.

"Best two out of three?" he asked.

Relief flooded through her. "What are the stakes? How about we make it worth my time?"

"Okay. Loser has to kiss the winner."

Her heart fluttered. "What about the winner?"

"Winner gets a kiss from the loser."

"Sucker bet."

"Take it or leave it."

They finished the game in less than five minutes. Kimberly was nervous, but she maintained her control of the cue and beat him easily. "I win."

"I guess that means I have to kiss you," he replied.

"Well, if it's not too much trouble."

"Where do you want it?"

Kimberly looked around. The game room was packed. It was Friday night. Kids were lined up waiting for the pool table, staring at them.

Not here, she thought. It would be embarrassing. And this is special—and—and—

Swallowing hard, she motioned for him to come close to her. He leaned down and she pressed herself into his arms, her heart thundering at the very thought of his lips. Then they touched. The kiss was amazing. More than she could ever have imagined. The world seemed to fall away. She no longer felt worried that people were watching them. In fact, she *liked* having an audience.

They parted, breathing hard. Griff took her hand and led her out of the game room, through the club, and outside, to his Tempo. The parking lot was dark. Griff opened the passenger side of the car first, closed it after she got in, then came around and climbed in the driver's side.

"Where are we going?" she asked as he shut the door.

"Wherever you want to go."

She looked around. There were no other kids milling about outside. "This looks good."

"I was just thinking that."

He came to her and she kissed him greedily. Her hunger for him was greater than it had ever been for a boy. She had never actually "made out" before. She was worried that she would be awkward and clumsy, or that she would ask stupid, embarrassing questions and reveal how naive and immature she was. But this, like everything else with Griff, was perfectly natural. She could not have felt more at ease.

The moment came when his mouth opened and she felt his probing tongue against her lips. Trembling, she opened her mouth slightly, felt his tongue move between her lips, then opened her mouth wide and gave in to him. Her heart pounded and her fingertips went numb. Never in her life had she felt *anything* like this.

Griff pulled away from her, his own chest heaving. "Wow," he said. "I mean, am I wrong, or was that a *wow*?"

"You're not wrong," Kimberly managed to say, both amused by his wide-eyed, schoolboy delivery, and aroused by his gentlemanly attempt at self-restraint. "Wow."

Kimberly launched herself at him, driving her tongue into his mouth. They kissed and caressed until a car door opened somewhere close. Kimberly scrambled out of Griff's arms and looked up to see another couple walking to the club. They had parked next to Griff's red car and were not looking back. The heat that had suffused Kimberly was now dulled enough for her to need a breather. Griff sensed this and did not push the issue. He sat back and held her hand.

She suddenly felt unduly self-conscious. Pulling down her sun visor, Kimberly found the small mirror and studied her face. Her makeup was holding up pretty well, but her hair was all over the place. Reaching for her purse, she drew out a brush and went to work on herself.

"Do you think my hair would look better if I did this?" She pulled it over to one side and let it drape down to cover part of her face. She could barely see out of one eye. Still, she considered it an interesting look. Very chic.

"I don't know," he said, a slight discomfort in his voice. "You look—"

"How about this?" she asked, pulling her hair back so severely that it made her look like a woman in a Robert Palmer video. "A little more makeup and it would be perfect."

Griff bit his lip.

"You hate it," she said, releasing her hair and allowing it to fall back into its natural state.

"I don't *hate* it. But you're stunning the way you are. Don't you know that?"

"You're just saying that."

Griff shook his head. "I just don't believe in asking anyone to change themselves for me. And I wouldn't appreciate having someone ask *me* to become somebody different for her. I don't make myself over for anyone. People just have to accept me for who and what I am. If they can't handle that, they don't have to hang around me."

"Are you mad?"

"What? Are you kidding? No, not at all."

Kimberly frowned. He might not have been angry, but, for some reason, *she* was. She didn't really want to change herself to please him but to amuse *herself*. *He* had been the one to decide she was simply trying to make herself more sexy for him. That had been a part of it, certainly, but a small part. She liked the idea of becoming someone new, of looking and feeling different. Sharon Cruise had learned not to mess with Kimberly the way she was now. But Kimberly wanted to make sure she didn't slip back, and once again become easy prey for Sharon or others like her. She wanted to make a clear statement. Griff had turned it all around and made it about *him*.

Turning to face him, Kimberly was about to let him know exactly how wrong he had been to go off without asking her *why* she wanted to change her appearance when she saw the pools of his perfect brown eyes and became lost in them. She was being foolish. He had misunderstood. Anyone could do that. And what he had said was wonderful. He accepted her for who she was. She didn't have to put on a show to please him.

"Griff?"

"Hey, look, I didn't mean—"

"Shut up and kiss me."

He did this gladly. Suddenly, a rapping came at the side window. Kimberly was startled. Fear burrowed into her with the inhuman cruelty of a power drill. She thought it was Gregory Rose and his friends. Or perhaps the hawk-nosed owner of the club. It turned out to be neither.

Staring into Griff's window was a young, dark-haired police officer. He had a square jaw, black curly hair, a bushy mustache, soulful eyes, and a trim but muscular build. Griff hurriedly rolled down the window.

"I'm Officer Murphy with the Cooper Hollow Sheriff's Department. Are you Joel Griffiths?"

Griff nodded. Kimberly looked around and saw a total of three police cruisers in the lot. Their car was surrounded by officers with hard faces. The young, black-haired cop had his hand on the butt of his weapon.

"I'd like to talk to you. If you would please get out of the car, Joel. And keep your hands where I can see them. You too, miss . . ."

Fourteen

"What's this all about?" Griff asked.

"Please get out of the car slowly and keep your hands in view at all times. Miss, if you could leave your purse on the frontseat?"

Griff turned to Kimberly and whispered, "Do what he says."

Kimberly nodded, terrified. The thought of defying these people had never entered her mind. Soon, both Griff and Kimberly were out of the car. Officers moved forward, and Griff was asked to turn around and place his hands on the car. A black-haired female officer with green eyes and the nametag "Montoya" patted Kimberly down and asked if she could look in Kimberly's purse.

"Yeah, sure, I guess."

"Please reach into the car slowly, take out the purse, and open it for me."

As Kimberly did as she was asked, she noted how incredibly polite the officers were acting. No, *polite* wasn't it at all. They were mannered, extremely aware of their tone, self-conscious of their actions. They didn't want to make any mistakes. What was happening here?

Officer Montoya looked inside Kimberly's bag with a penlight, nodded to another officer, and told Kimberly she could close it. The officers shined their flashlights into the car, looked at the seats, then backed away.

"It would be great to know what was going on here," Griff said, unable to erase the tremor from his voice.

Kimberly was allowed to come around the front of the car and stand beside him. Her hand slipped into his.

"We'd like you to come down and answer some questions," the first cop said. He had a male model's face, complete with a cleft chin and perfect cheekbones.

"Am I under arrest?" Griff asked.

"No. We just have a very important matter we'd like to discuss with you. We'd appreciate your cooperation."

"Yeah, okay," Griff said. "I'll come down."

"We'll need to contact your parents."

Griff gave them the number. "It's just my mom. Go easy on her, okay? Don't scare her, she gets rattled easy."

"Don't worry," Officer Murphy said flatly.

Turning to Kimberly, Griff asked, "Can you call your aunt or uncle to come get you?"

"I'm going with you. I'm not staying here."

"It's not going to be much of a date."

"I'm going."

Griff nodded. "Why don't you drive my car down?"

"We're assigning an officer to stay with your vehicle," Officer Murphy said.

"I really want to know what's going on," Griff said, his tone indicating that he could become difficult if he didn't get answers soon.

"There's a detective downtown who would like to speak to you," Officer Murphy said as he withdrew a laminated card. "I'm going to read you your rights. This does not mean you're under arrest. It's important for you to be aware of what's entitled to you."

"But if I'm not under arrest—"

The officer read the full text on the card, asking Griff if he understood his rights as they had been explained to him. Griff said that he did, and Officer Murphy ushered Griff and Kimberly into the backseat of his cruiser. Dozens of teens had come out of the club to watch the scene. Kimberly doubted that any would notice Griff's lack of handcuffs. He was not being arrested; he was only going to the station to answer some questions. Few would make the distinction, she was certain.

The drive to the police station was quiet. Griff held Kimberly's hand. There was little either of them could say. They were both terrified.

In less than a half hour they reached the station and were ushered inside. Kimberly was asked to sit in a small waiting area while Griff was led away to be questioned. She wished there was something she could do or say to make this nightmare better for him. Perhaps just being here would be enough.

She prayed that it would.

Kimberly wandered through now familiar woods, the tiny hand of a child in hers. Comforting words flowed from her, stilling the fears of the little girl she had brought with her. The child had curly black hair, braces, and a Cindy Crawford mole beside the crook of her mouth. She was dressed in an NYU sweatshirt that grazed her ankles. Her feet were bare and bloody. Kimberly barely noticed.

They reached the clearing where the gray horse waited. The magnificent animal swiveled its head in her direction. She read a world of meaning in its wide dark eyes. She could almost hear the words, "Give me what I need and I'll give you what you need."

She picked up the child, who had begun to kick and scream, and carried her to the horse.

A hand descended on Kimberly's shoulder, waking her from the dream. She jumped, her fear giving way to embarrassment. She had fallen asleep in the police station's waiting area. Kimberly looked down at the hand on her shoulder. It was bone white and luminous. The sleeve of a lacy dress bit at the wrist. A strange ring sat on the wedding finger. Water dripped from the hand.

Kimberly recoiled and looked and looked up to see Griff's warm, smiling face. Her eyes darted back to her shoulder. The hand touching her belonged to her boyfriend.

"What's going on?" Kimberly asked, wiping the grit from the corners of her eyes.

"Let's get out of here, first," Griff said. "I'll tell you about it in the car."

78

Kimberly saw that Griff was not alone. A woman in a navy business suit stood behind him. His mother. The resemblance was undeniable. Joel's mother was close to fifty and very attractive. The navy suit she wore may have fit perfectly a few years ago, but it was now a little snug. Her graying hair was set perfectly, though.

Kimberly rose quickly, realizing that this was not the ideal way to meet someone's mother. The older woman seemed aware of this. She smiled and Kimberly felt instantly relieved.

After rushed introductions, they hurried from the police station. In moments, Kimberly was being ushered into the backseat of Mrs. Griffiths' car. Griff slid in beside her.

"I'll drop you off at home," the older woman offered. "Where do you live?"

Kimberly winced. Griff apparently had not explained Kimberly's home situation to his mother. Earlier that evening, Tanya had driven Kimberly to the club. Going out with another girl was acceptable to Uncle David and Aunt Margaret. If they had known that Kimberly was meeting a boy at the club, an argument of apocalyptic proportions might have taken place. Should they see Mrs. Griffiths and her son, instead of Tanya, letting Kimberly off, she would have quite a bit of explaining to do.

There was an easy solution. She would have Mrs. Griffiths drop her off a block before her house. Griff and his mother didn't know where she lived. They would never realize the difference. After they were gone, she would walk home. Kimberly told her the name of a street and they pulled into traffic.

"Tell me what happened," Kimberly said urgently.

A ragged breath escaped Griff as he said, "Gregory Rose is dead. They found his body a couple of hours ago."

Kimberly felt as if she had been struck. Griff had obviously been through too much to couch the words. Once the initial shock faded, however, Kimberly found that she was having a hard time stifling a smile.

Dead. Actually dead. She had never seen a dead person. The idea carried little reality to her beyond what she had witnessed on television and at the movies.

Kimberly had attended her parents' memorial service, but her experience was not the same as those of her friends who described open casket services. Her parents had died in an explosion. There were no bodies for the caskets. Kimberly had never been granted the luxury of saying goodbye that way. In a way, she was glad. She would not have wanted to see her mother and father in caskets, lying stiff, waxy and made up. It sounded horrible beyond imagination.

Because she had never seen them dead, it sometimes seemed to Kimberly that they had simply *gone away*. A part of her had always been able to imagine them coming through the front door again, alive and whole. Without warning, Griff's words from the other night came to her: *My father was dead. I didn't feel anything but relief. Pretty terrible, huh?*

No. It wasn't terrible. Kimberly gingerly touched her jaw. She was still nursing the bruise Rose had given her. Griff had been gentle when they had kissed, but the soreness and the pain had not completely abated. The ugly purple welt would be there for some time.

Rose was dead. *Good.*

Kimberly shuddered and chided herself, but nothing completely erased the tide of satisfaction and relief that had washed over her at the news. Nothing except the sobering thought of Griff being accused of Rose's murder.

No one had said murder, of course, but how could it have been anything else with a monster like Gregory Rose?

"Why did they go after you?" Kimberly asked, outraged. "From what I've heard, there's a dozen people in this town who would have liked to see that piece of garbage dead."

Griff stared at her, obviously taken back by the ferocity of her words. Slowly, he said, "They found my sister's

80

necklace on his body. People saw me arguing with Rose in the club. And, as I found out tonight, Rose hit you."

Kimberly winced. "I would have told you about it, Griff, but we didn't know each other at all that night. Then, when I saw the way the two of you were going at it, I just thought—"

"I know," he said as he took her hand and gave it a gentle squeeze. "Don't worry about it."

Kimberly nodded. "You don't have an alibi, do you?"

"I was out driving. Mom and I had had a fight. A couple of the neighbors saw me drive off about an hour before Rose was killed. I came back two hours later."

"You were just out driving," Kimberly repeated dully. She believed him, but she realized how weak that alibi would sound to someone who didn't know Griff. "What are you gonna do?"

From the front seat, Mrs. Griffiths offered, "I know a few lawyers. I'll be phoning them tonight."

Kimberly considered mentioning that her uncle was a lawyer, then thought better of it.

They reached Kimberly's part of town much faster than she would have liked. There was still so much to talk about.

"Looks like there's some trouble up ahead," Mrs. Griffiths said.

Kimberly looked up sharply. As they drove onto her street, her vision was stunned by the flashing red lights of fire engines and the raised voices of a crowd gathered directly before her smoking house.

Fifteen

"Trouble" was an understatement. Fire units and two ambulances were parked in the street. Mrs. Griffiths had barely stopped the car before Kimberly burst from it and ran to the crowd of figures standing on the spacious front lawn. Uncle David and Aunt Margaret wore expensive evening clothes. They had told Kimberly that they would be driving into the city for a dinner meeting. They had apparently just arrived home; their clothes bore no signs of smoke or soot.

Kimberly bit her lip. The upstairs window from which smoke was wafting was *her bedroom* window. Whatever blaze had occurred must have been quickly contained. The rest of the house seemed untouched.

Strong arms enfolded Kimberly from behind as she tried to run for the front door. The man who caught her wore a shiny yellow coat and smelled of smoke and ash. Images of racing toward her parents' smoking restaurant and being held back in just this way by another stranger exploded in her mind.

The fight went out of Kimberly the moment she saw the stern faces of her aunt and uncle. The fireman unlocked his arms from her waist and quickly stepped away.

David Kilpatrick was a handsome, brown-haired man with a square jaw and a weightlifter's body. His wife was a tall, slender California blonde with a pretty face that belied a hardness of spirit. Margaret worked out religiously and ate very little. Except, that is, when she was dining out, and trying to make an impression.

A police officer followed the couple, his notepad out. "So you don't have any idea who might have wanted to

82

cause you harm?" he asked.

"Someone who didn't like the size of their bill, probably," David Kilpatrick said. "I *am* a lawyer, after all. You know what they say. The first thing you do is kill all the lawyers."

"This is serious," the police officer said.

"I know. So do your job and find out who's responsible. If I think of anything else I'll get back to you."

The officer slapped his notepad shut in frustration and walked off.

"Uncle David?" Kimberly asked. The man ignored her.

They don't care, Kimberly realized. They don't want to hear me, they don't want to see me, they don't want to know I'm around. "Uncle David—"

With a frown, Margaret tapped her husband on the shoulder. "Honey. The girl needs something."

Her aunt's words cut through Kimberly. *The girl.* To Aunt Margaret, she was always just "the girl."

"What is it, Kimberly?" Uncle David said in exasperation.

Kimberly stared up at the window to her bedroom and thought of her precious photo albums filled with pictures of her real parents. "How bad was it? Is there anything left of my room?"

"I have no idea," he said, distracted by something that was happening behind Kimberly.

Kimberly jumped as she felt a hand descend on her shoulder. It was Griff and his mother. In the shock of finding that her room had burned she had forgotten they were still around.

Kimberly's uncle waved at Griff, then at Kimberly. He was on the edge of really losing it, in Kimberly's estimation. That made them pretty evenly matched.

"Would someone like to explain *this* crap?" David Kilpatrick asked.

Before Kimberly or Griff could speak, Mrs. Griffiths introduced herself. Kimberly's guardians just stared at her.

"It seems we've both had some shocks this evening," Mrs. Griffiths said. "At least everyone seems to be all right."

"Kimberly?" David asked. "Do you *know* these people?"

Realizing that there was no way around the truth, Kimberly told her guardians that she and Griff had been out on a date. She did not explain how they had joined up with Griff's mother.

"Then you lied to us," David said slowly, a dangerous momentum creeping into his speech. "You snuck around behind our backs to see this *boy*. That's fine, Kimberly. That's just wonderful. We're going to have to have a little *talk* about this—"

Before the shouting could begin, the officer who had been speaking to Uncle David before appeared. "Mr. Kilpatrick, we know what started the fire."

"Fine, what was it?" Kimberly's uncle asked coolly.

The officer held up the remains of a pack of cigarettes. "Someone had been smoking in the bedroom. A lit cigarette was tossed into the wastepaper basket, the rest is history. The fire marshal said it's a miracle the entire house wasn't demolished."

"What's it look like in the bedroom?" Kimberly asked.

"Totaled," the man said, then excused himself as a fireman called for him.

Kimberly felt her heart ache. Her photo albums were gone.

"So," Aunt Margaret said, "first she almost burns the house down with her cigarettes, then—"

"*What are you talking about?*" Kimberly cried. "I don't *smoke.*"

"Well, don't look at *us,*" Aunt Margaret said. "You know damn well we're both too health conscious to suck on those cancer sticks. And the fire was in *your* room."

"I didn't, I wouldn't have, I—" Kimberly sputtered.

Griff finally broke his silence. "Mr. Kilpatrick, you know there has to be some other explanation."

84

Uncle David advanced on Griff, driving him back as if by sheer force of will. "You, son, had better learn your place, and you had better learn quickly."

"My place?" Griff asked, his expression darkening.

Kimberly had seen this before. She wanted to warn Griff not to take the bait, but it was too late for that.

"This world is very simple," Mr. Kilpatrick said, his eyes practically on fire. "There are two kinds of people. Those who have and those who want. I can tell which kind *you* are from the way you've been looking at my niece."

"You can, can you?" Griff asked, his anger mounting.

"Excuse me," Mrs. Griffiths said, breaking in, "I don't know who in the hell you think you are, mister, and I don't care. But it's obvious to me that you've got a lot to learn about people."

"Please, don't," Kimberly said, tears welling in her eyes. But she was invisible. She always became invisible with her aunt and uncle. Just as she had been invisible to her parents on the day they died . . .

"I know a lot more than you'll ever know," David said. "I deal with all kinds, every day. I can spot *your* kind coming a mile off."

Shuddering, Mrs. Griffiths said, "And I know *your* kind, Mr. Kilpatrick. I was married to a man just like you until he drank himself into the grave."

Uncle David stared at Griff's mother. He was not used to anyone speaking to him in such a bold way.

Mrs. Griffiths ignored his angry glare. "I've only just met your Kimberly and already I can tell that she's not the kind of girl who would have done what you're accusing her of doing. As to her sneaking around behind your back so that she can see my son—which I now wish I had known beforehand—maybe she wouldn't *have* to do such things if you would just shut up long enough to *listen* to her."

"Don't even *think* about telling me how to run my household!" Uncle David shouted.

Griff launched himself at the man. Two fireman grabbed him before he could get his hands on Kimberly's uncle.

"Don't you *ever* come around here," Uncle David threatened. "Don't you ever come anywhere near my niece again. Is that understood?"

"I'll do whatever the hell I want," Griff answered.

"Stop it, stop it!" Kimberly cried, but no one was listening.

"Yeah, well, you're going to have a hard time getting anywhere near her after this." David turned to Kimberly. "You can forget about your weekend passes from now until you graduate."

"Uncle David, no!" Kimberly pleaded. She turned to Griff but there was little he could do. The men who were holding him then let him go and quickly left.

"I don't want to deal with any more of this tonight," Kimberly's uncle said tensely. "We're going to get a hotel room in the city. In the morning, you go back to the school."

"I want my jewelry." Margaret shuddered. "I don't want my jewelry left here. Anyone could just walk off with it."

"All right," he said. "I'll see what I can do."

"Uncle David," Kimberly said, attempting to draw her uncle's attention. "Please . . . !"

"Say your goodbyes to your little boyfriend," he said as he took his wife's hand and dragged her away. He vanished into the mass of people surrounding the house.

Kimberly turned and melted into Griff's embrace.

"Meet me at the club Monday night," he whispered. "My Mom'll be okay about this. She'll help. I know she will."

Relief flooded through Kimberly. She wouldn't be able to see Griff on the weekends, but she could sneak out during the week.

"I will," Kimberly said, then kissed him goodbye.

Twenty minutes after Griff and his mother had gone,

Kimberly wandered through the crowd, doing her best to avoid her guardians. A snippet of conversation sliced through the fog that had settled over her thoughts:

". . . the brightest red you'd ever see. I swear, it hasn't been since that Cauley child had his hotrod that I'd seen anything like that parked on this street . . .

"Was it like that one? A Ferrari?" a second woman asked.

"Just like it. Fire red, to boot. Parked in front of my place for close to an hour. Then it peeled out just before the smoke started. I was the one who called the fire department, you know."

"You don't say."

Kimberly suddenly found it difficult to breathe.

Sharon Cruise drove a red Ferrari. She lived three counties away, but she had claimed to be sick today and had been allowed to go home early for the weekend. She would have had plenty of time to drive to Cooper Hollow and set the fire.

Kimberly did not volunteer this information to anyone though she knew that she should turn Sharon in. This was serious. Someone could have been hurt in the fire, perhaps even killed. Maybe even her.

Would anyone listen to her? It wasn't likely. Not here, anyway. Here, she was invisible. But back at Cooper, she could make things happen.

Kimberly was consumed by her anger for Sharon. Griff would not have killed Gregory Rose, but the police saw things differently. He would need her to be with him, to support him. Now, because of Sharon, their time together would amount to a few stolen hours a week. Nothing more.

Images of her parents ran through her head. All she had had left of them were the photographs. Sharon had destroyed them.

Hugging herself, Kimberly decided that there would be time to deal with Sharon properly.

All the time in the world.

Sixteen

The weekend passed slowly and painfully. Kimberly attempted to escape by immersing herself in her studies, but it was no good. Her concentration slid after only a few minutes. She could not resist daydreams in which she snapped Sharon Cruise's neck like a dried branch. Nevertheless, she managed to complete the minimum amount of work that had been required by her teachers, some ten hours worth on Saturday and Sunday.

Ashlyn had remained at school. She was quiet and strangely mournful when Kimberly saw her Sunday after her guardians dropped her off. Though Gregory Rose had treated her monstrously, she seemed to be sorry for his loss. After a single, demonically animated conversation about the best way to get back at Sharon Cruise for all she had done to Kimberly, Ashlyn had fallen back into a dark mood. Ashlyn's silences had made it clear to Kimberly that her friend needed to be alone.

On Sunday night, just before lights out, Ashlyn entered Kimberly's room. Her eyes were wild. She was covered in sweat.

"Let's do it," Ashlyn said crazily. "Tomorrow. Let's get the little witch!"

Before Kimberly could reply, Ashlyn blew out of her room like a sudden, violent wind.

Monday morning, they chose the course of their vengeance. If everything went according to plan, Sharon would be expelled when it was all over. She might even face criminal charges.

It was going to be a wonderful day.

An hour before dinner, during the free period following the afternoon riding class, Ashlyn and Kimberly went over their preparations one last time. The stunt they were pulling was risky. If anything went wrong, Kimberly could end up seriously injured.

But nothing would go wrong. Kimberly knew that. She possessed a certainty about this plan that she had never felt about any plan before.

She thought about Griff. He would never approve of what they were going to do to Sharon. That was all right. He didn't have to approve. In fact, he would never know the truth behind what was about to happen. Not unless Ashlyn told, and Kimberly trusted her friend to keep silent. After all, they would be equally guilty when it was done.

Thoughts of Griff were the only things capable of driving out Kimberly's fantasies of vengeance against Sharon. She wanted desperately to call him, but had no access to a phone. She had never felt so cut off. Before meeting Ashlyn and then Griff, the isolation at Cooper had almost been a blessing. After all, the outside world contained Uncle David and Aunt Margaret. Now, the isolation was becoming a problem.

"Are you ready?" Ashlyn asked as she approached.

The late afternoon sun was in Kimberly's eyes. "You know it."

They went over the plan one last time. Kimberly had insisted that whatever they do should center around riding. They had agreed that tampering with Sharon's equipment was too dangerous. A riding accident could prove crippling or fatal. Neither of them wanted murder on their conscience. Besides, each student was charged with the responsibility of checking their equipment before getting astride. If they had sawed through Sharon's reins so that they would break at a crucial moment, Sharon would discover the tampering and an investigation would ensue.

Instead, Kimberly had chosen to tamper with her

own equipment and make it look as if Sharon had been the one at fault. Everyone knew that Ms. Saberhagen, their instructor, was always getting on Kimberly because she almost never checked her equipment. This time, she would purposely forget and fall victim to an accident, one that she and Ashlyn would stage. Several stacks of hay were piled up outside the riding house. Kimberly would fall into these.

"All right," Ashlyn said. "Come around to the hay stack. When you're ready for it, dig in and make Centurion buck. As he goes up, let go of the good rein and yank on the bad one. It'll break, you'll fall, but the hay will break your fall. I'll make enough noise to get everyone's attention. Got it?"

"No problem," Kimberly said, though she was becoming a little worried.

"Hey," Ashlyn said, "look at that. Sharon's riding into the cemetery again."

"Fitting," Kimberly replied, then allowed her friend to help her onto her mount. "All things considered."

Sharon Cruise rode through one of the neatly marked paths around the school grounds. She thought it was almost funny the way it had all come around, all come back to her. When it began, the only pleasure that skinny little reject Kimberly had in life was the time she spent riding. Only during those brief but wondrous moments was she free from the torment that had become her life. Astride, with the wind whistling through her hair, the cool breeze of twilight caressing her face with its tantalizing fingers, the reject had escaped the laughter and the ridicule.

Now, it was Sharon's turn. Her entire life had been turned inside out. The only refuge she could find was out here, in the open, galloping wildly through the greens.

Nothing made sense anymore. Nothing!

Sharon entered the graveyard. The riding trail

through the cemetery was narrow and winding. Only seniors who were experienced riders were allowed to guide their mounts through the small city of the dead trapped within the school grounds. Sharon did not slow her mount. Instead, she drove the black horse she rode into a greater fury. Together, they had run this course dozens of times before. Her teachers had frowned on her recklessness and had lectured her endlessly.

As always, however, Sharon did exactly as she pleased.

It occurred to her now that she had never ridden through the trail at a slow gait. Not once had she dismounted to look at the beautiful tombstones and the loving epitaphs carved upon the stones. Not once had she really seen the sharp corners of the unyielding white stones, their razor-like edges.

Suddenly, a shape appeared before Sharon. It darted out from behind a monument to her left. A horse. A towering, gray horse with blood-red eyes and steaming breath. Strange. It wasn't cold enough for breath to turn to steam. Now the hulking creature was larger than the monument that had hidden it before. The horse was growing before her eyes, expanding like a balloon. Insane, impossible, almost comedic in its absurdity. Nevertheless, it was real and it had crossed her path and stopped.

Sharon's mount came to a sudden halt and reared up, whinnying in terror. She grabbed hold of her reins, certain they would snap. They held. Grasping the reins harder than she thought possible, Sharon squeezed her legs against either side of her mount and prayed that she would not be thrown off.

Only a few feet away, the nightmare horse's lips pulled back in a macabre grimace. The flesh above its teeth rippled as if it were being buffeted by fabulous winds. The creature's teeth had been sharpened into points. Blood leaked from the crevices between its massive, unnatural maw, and a scream unlike any sound made by man or beast came from the monster.

Sharon felt a terrible pain in her jaw. She realized that she was clenching her teeth together in response to the horrible scream leaping from the mouth of the gray horse. For an instant, she was certain that her heart had stopped. It came to her in those final seconds, as her black mount toppled over to one side and the unyielding surface of a white marble monument reached up for her head, that her horse had literally been frightened to death. Sharon screamed as her head was driven into the cold stone. The initial impact brought a burst of pain then a merciful blanket of unconsciousness as the corpse of her horse collapsed upon her, crushing her against the tombstone.

Seventeen

Kimberly witnessed the entire accident. She saw Sharon race into the cemetery and saw her encounter the gray horse from her own awful dreams. The cry of the nightmarish animal seared Kimberly's brain. She was surprised that her own mount had not risen up in response to the terrible sound.

Kimberly's teacher, Jane Saberhagen, had been only fifty feet away when Sharon's mount had risen. She had looked up in alarm, but to Kimberly's mind, her expression was not sufficiently horror-struck. The teacher's horse had only shifted a bit at the sound.

Didn't they see it? Kimberly thought desperately. Didn't they hear it? Didn't they? What's wrong with them? Were they blind? Deaf? Were they *crazy?*

The short, middle-aged woman commanded her mount to bolt in the direction of the graveyard.

"Ms. Saberhagen!" Kimberly cried, anxious to give some kind of warning. But when she looked back to the cemetery, the gray horse was gone.

Students raced across the grounds on foot and on horseback. Kimberly and Ms. Saberhagen were the first to arrive. They encountered the twisted mass of blood and shattered limbs that had been Sharon Cruise and turned away instantly at the sight. There was no point in checking the body. Sharon couldn't have survived that. No one could.

Kimberly found herself looking back to Sharon's body. The dead girl lay beneath her mount, the wreckage of a once beautiful tombstone tumbled around her. This was the first dead body she had ever seen. She was disgusted at the sight. The blood seemed to rush from her head and she found it difficult to breathe. Still, she couldn't quite bring herself to look away.

This was what you wanted, wasn't it? an oddly soothing voice whispered from deep within her mind.

No, Kimberly thought. This has nothing to do with me.

Even if that's true, Sharon's dead and gone. She's paid for what she's done to you. Happy?

She wasn't happy. In fact, now that she was over the initial shock, Kimberly felt nothing. No glee, no satisfaction, and no remorse. She was not even sickened by the bloody display, as so many of the others had been.

Kimberly looked away and surveyed the faces of the students who had gathered in the cemetery. Not all of them were broken up over Sharon's death, or repulsed by the blood and gore. Several of them seemed fascinated by it all. Kimberly saw that Ashlyn had suddenly appeared. She wasn't looking at Sharon. Her eyes were trained on Kimberly. Her expression was unreadable. Somehow, it unnerved Kimberly more than the sight of Sharon's mangled body. She felt as if her reaction to this event was important, as if she were being scrutinized, as if it were some kind of test.

Or Initiation.

Kimberly turned away. After a few minutes, Elise Chalmers, the school's headmistress, appeared. She was a tall, immaculately groomed woman in her late forties. Her clothing was stylish and fresh. She seemed to have stepped out of a high fashion magazine.

"What happened?" Ms. Chalmers cried. Ms. Saberhagen explained that Sharon had been riding too quickly through the cemetery. Something had caused her horse to rise up. The two adults began to question the students who had witnessed the accident. No one had seen what had spooked Sharon's horse. When it was Kimberly's turn to be questioned, she repeated the story the other girls had told.

"A small animal of some kind," Ms. Saberhagen said dully, attempting to lose herself in the recitation of a

94

reasonable explanation for the awful accident. "It doesn't happen often, but it happens. The animal must have run into Sharon's path and the horse bucked. The fall alone doesn't seem to have been enough to kill the horse. I'd say it had a heart attack."

Ms. Chalmers was shaken. Her skin, normally vibrant, had gone pale. "There's a lot we have to do here." Turning, Ms. Chalmers addressed those who had gathered at the site. The students who had witnessed the accident were ordered back to the school. They were instructed not to say anything about the accident. They were told that an emergency assembly would be called in an hour.

Kimberly fell in with the numbed mass of students. The silence Ms. Chalmers had demanded remained intact until they were halfway to the school, then the chattering began. By the time they reached the school, Kimberly was certain the news would spread at a fabulous speed. Ms. Chalmers didn't need to bother with her assembly. Everyone would know about Sharon's death within the hour.

Of course, none of them would know the *truth*, and that made all the difference in the world.

The truth? the voice in her head asked. *And what exactly is the truth?*

I know what I saw, Kimberly thought.

Oh? And what was that? A creature from your dreams? Something that no one else heard or saw? If you want to be laughed at or sent away for counseling, tell someone that. Hell, you could even leave the school tonight, go to the police and tell them. How does that sound?

Stupid, Kimberly thought. Of course, stupid. What else could it be?

Kimberly had not walked back with Ashlyn. Her friend was waiting for her in her room.

"I don't know what to say," Ashlyn whispered impassively. "If it had been anyone else I guess I'd say it was a real shame or something. I don't know. I don't know what to say."

95

Kimberly hesitated. She was the only one to have seen the gray horse. Maybe her mind *was* playing tricks on her. Maybe Sharon's accident *had* been caused by something else; an animal running into the horse's path was only *one* possibility.

"Where are Tanya and Nikki?" Kimberly asked, suddenly picturing one or both of the remaining Predators crouching behind a tombstone, loosing a frightened animal at precisely the right moment.

"In the study hall. Why?"

Kimberly shook her head. The thought had been ridiculous. "No reason. I'll tell you, though. I just had this really weird thought. It's really bad."

"What is it?"

"I'm just wondering—what do we do now?"

Ashlyn nodded. She understood Kimberly's meaning. With Sharon out of their lives they had nothing on which to focus their attention. "Try and survive our tests this week, I suppose," she answered.

"Tests," Kimberly said numbly, suddenly recalling the major exams she was facing on Friday.

Kimberly hugged herself. A girl was dead. A human life had been extinguished. It should have *meant* something to her, something more than the casual curiosity of whether or not their tests might be postponed because of the inevitable shock waves caused by the accident.

Horribly, it did not.

Eighteen

Kimberly waited until after lights out and then left the school on her own. The long walk through the woods invigorated her and when she finally saw the familiar blue light in the distance, she practically ran the rest of the way to the Night Owl Club. She noticed Griff's Tempo in the parking lot before stepping inside.

Griff waited at the same table they had shared on their first date. He rose and took her into his arms. Kimberly had no idea how long the embrace lasted, but she was grateful that he did not try to pull away. She needed to be held.

"I love you," he whispered.

Startled, she hugged him tighter. "Me, too."

They pulled away from one another and sat down. Jenny, the blond-haired waitress, came by and took their orders. The club was trying something new — vanilla and cherry colas, fifties style. Kimberly thought it would be fun to try a vanilla cola. When it arrived moments later, she tasted it and knew she made the right choice.

Part of her wanted to talk more about their feelings for each other. Griff had admitted that he loved her. She had admitted the same feeling for him. Still, they were so new to each other and Kimberly didn't want to push things any faster than they were already going. It was enough that they had spoken those special words.

"You seem pretty charged up," Griff noted.

Kimberly felt something in her chest tighten. "What do you mean?"

Griff shrugged. He took a sip from his cherry cola.

"Nothing *bad*. You seem happy, that's all."

"Am I allowed?" Kimberly asked, unaware of the sarcastic edge to her voice until the words had escaped.

"Of course you're allowed," Griff said, concern lacing his tone. "I was just wondering what happened today. You really seem cheered up. I thought maybe something good happened."

Kimberly reached out and took his hand, squeezing it firmly. "I'm sorry I overreaceed," she said.

"It's okay," he answered, his bright smile returning. He caressed her hand as they sipped their drinks.

In spite of Griff's attentions, Kimberly's wonderful mood evaporated. She felt as if she had woken from a comforting sleep. The reality was that someone had died and she felt better than she had in weeks. What was she, some kind of *ghoul?* Even Sharon Cruise deserved some pity.

Her thoughts went back to the fire Sharon had set in her room at home. Kimberly could have been in the house when the fire started. The flames were *supposed* to have gone out of control and consumed everything. Sharon wouldn't have felt any remorse if *Kimberly* had died; she had probably hoped for Kimberly's death. *Why should* she *worry about feeling nothing for Sharon?*

Kimberly shifted in her seat. Sharon had destroyed the one thing that had been more important to Kimberly than anything else: the photo albums of her parents. Now she had only the one picture in her dresser drawer at school.

A touch of resentment toward Griff crept into Kimberly and she pulled her hand away from his. He winced, as if she had hurt him. Kimberly had to restrain a smile. A small voice cried, *he deserves some punishment for ruining your good mood. Now you're even so you can get on with your evening.*

"Have you heard anything from the police?" Kimberly asked, deciding that if Griff could bring up unpleasant subjects, she could, too.

"No," he said, his features darkening.

Kimberly suddenly felt terrible for the game she had just played, even if she had only been playing it in her own head. Griff loved her. He *needed* her. She leaned forward and kissed him across the table.

"What was that for?" he asked, once again confused, but this time pleasantly so.

"Because I love you, too," she said, the words coming much easier than she had anticipated. "And I'll be here for you. I just wanted you to know that."

He smiled. "Same here." An awkward, boyish expression crept across his face. "This is going to sound like a stupid question, but—"

"There's no such thing. Just ask."

"Kimberly, if you could have anything in the world, anything at all, what would it be?"

She hesitated. There was no way she could tell him what had popped into her mind. "Just to be with you."

"You've got that. Something else. Anything else."

"Anything?"

"Anything at all."

She knew what she wanted. The answer had leaped instantly into her thoughts: to see her parents again; to tell them that she was sorry and to beg their forgiveness. *That's* what she wanted, but that was impossible.

No, wait, there was something she wanted even more. The chance to go back and do it over. To have her parents with her now. That's what she wanted most dearly in life.

Kimberly stared down into her vanilla cola, swirling her straw around in her drink. "I don't know. I just don't know. I'm just happy to be here with you, okay?"

"Sure," Griff said. "I understand."

"You didn't kill Gregory Rose," Kimberly said abruptly.

"No, I didn't," Griff said.

"The police think you did."

"Yeah."

"Maybe the only way to get them to change their minds is to find out ourselves who did it."

Griff shook his head slowly. "You've been reading too many Nancy Drew mysteries. It doesn't work like that in real life."

Kimberly shuddered. She wasn't sure what upset her more. Griff's condescending remark or his willingness to give up without trying to fight what was happening.

"I'm sorry," Griff said quickly. "I phrased that wrong. What I mean is, I've been thinking about that, too. But the only way we can find out who killed Rose is to get into his life, and none of the people who knew him really well are going to talk to either of *us*."

Reluctantly, Kimberly nodded. "Then what do we do?"

"There's nothing we can do. Nothing except wait and hope that the police do their job and keep investigating. Obviously they don't have enough on me yet to press charges or else they'd have done it already. Maybe while they're trying to find more evidence against me they'll find the real murderer."

Once again, Kimberly felt frustrated and powerless, the same way she had felt when she stood before the burning restaurant where her parents had died, being held back by strangers because they knew nothing could be done. The same way she had felt the other night before the sight of her burned-out room.

"I know what we can do," Kimberly said suddenly, a mischievous smile reaching across her pretty face.

"What's that?"

"The same thing we were doing when we were interrupted the other night. I mean, your car *is* parked right outside. I saw it there myself."

"That's true."

"And there is such a thing as paying the bill and walking outside."

"Uh-huh."

"And unlocking the car."

"Yep."

"And getting inside."

"Oh, yeah."

They stared at each other with matching grins.

"I think," Kimberly said as she slid out of the booth and stood up, "the best way to put it is, 'run, don't walk.' "

He was fishing out his wallet as Kimberly raced him to the door. His arm went around her waist as she neared the front door and he handed a bill to the blond waitress, who was standing nearby.

"Hello," Kimberly said to the waitress, laughing joyously as Griff hugged her from behind.

"Hello," returned the waitress with raised eyebrows.

"Goodbye," they both said as Griff released her and they raced from the club.

Nineteen

The week passed quickly. Kimberly immersed herself in her studies. She was amazed at how easily she absorbed information. Never before had she been so at ease with her material. If she had worn glasses, she might have said she'd been going through life with a bad prescription, and now she had gotten it fixed and could suddenly see the world with amazing clarity.

The investment of the hours was unavoidable. She had not suddenly been granted the ability to speed read, or flip through a book and absorb all the information in seconds the way a robot might. In a way, though, she felt as if her brain *had* become a fully functioning super computer, able to deal with far greater challenges than her school books could throw at her.

Kimberly was glad to have something on which she could focus. Her worry over Griff and the Gregory Rose murder seized her whenever she tried to rest. Thinking about tests and homework allowed her to push from her mind visions of her boyfriend languishing in prison.

When she slept, though, she dreamt neither of Griff nor of school. Instead, she dreamed of the beautiful gray horse and the children she brought to it. She would laugh as the horse bolted, a child clinging to its mane. On some level, Kimberly knew that she should have found the dreams disturbing, but, always, in the morning, she felt comforting waves of satisfaction pour over her. And during the day, she felt strangely energized.

She had only one bad moment, and that was on Thursday, in Natural Studies. The class had just learned that in several cultures it was believed that when a person killed his enemy, he inherited the enemy's attributes. In other words, murder the fleetest of foot and you run like a gazelle. Take the life of a great strategist and no one will ever be able to out-think you on the field of battle.

Sharon, despite all of her negative aspects, had had one undeniably positive attribute: She had been brilliant in her studies.

Though haunted by this realization, Kimberly found that she was much happier and much more productive when she put aside any thoughts of Sharon. The public address Ms. Chalmers had promised had been performed, a psychiatric counselor had established a temporary office at the school, and students troubled by the accident were advised to seek her out. Those who had been affected the most by Sharon's death, the handful who had actually seen her ruined body, and those who had remained her friends, even after the Predators' cruel treatment of her had begun, were urged to make an appointment at the counselor's office. A few students whose behavior had changed radically since the accident were *ordered* to see her.

Again, pushing all disturbing thoughts of Sharon's death from her mind, Kimberly couldn't understand what the big deal was. She could see some people being a little shaken at first, but, she told herself, they should shrug it off, say to themselves, *better you than me*, and get on with their lives.

On Friday, after the last of her exams, Kimberly came back to her room to find Ashlyn waiting for her.

"I've got some good news," Ashlyn said cheerfully.

"What's that."

"You're not stuck here for the weekend after all."

"Yes, I am," Kimberly said wearily as she lay down on her bed and stretched. "Uncle David isn't about to call and tell Ms. Chalmers to let me out."

"Call, no. *Write*, yes."

Kimberly sat up, suddenly interested. "What'd you do?"

"I have friends on the outside," Ashlyn said as she removed an envelope from her jacket pocket. "This is just a duplicate. We'll burn it when you're through gawking at it."

Kimberly held out her hand and took the envelope from Ashlyn. It was on the stationery of her father's law firm and had been addressed to Ms. Chalmers. The envelope had even been postmarked.

She opened the envelope and read the enclosed letter. A smile blossomed on her face. The sheet of paper fell from her fingers and she rushed into Ashlyn's waiting arms.

"How did you *do* this?" Kimberly asked joyously. The letter was a perfect forgery. So perfect, in fact, even Kimberly would have been fooled if not for the letter's content. In it, her uncle gave permission for Kimberly to be released on a weekend pass and to stay with Tanya's family.

"I told you, friends on the outside."

A sudden, paralyzing fear coursed through Kimberly. "Ms. Chalmers is going to want confirmation on this. She's going to call Uncle David."

"Sure she will. Already has, actually."

"Then why are you still smiling?"

"Look at the phone number at the top."

Kimberly had not taken in the number before. She picked up the sheet of paper and studied it more closely.

"Get it, now?" Ashlyn asked brightly.

The number was not for her uncle's office.

"No, I don't get it," Kimberly said.

"Actors. They work cheap. If they're desperate enough, they don't ask questions. I've got two of them in an office in Manhattan. Ms. Chalmers calls the number on the stationery. I mean, she's not going to go through all the trouble of looking up your uncle's

phone number, not when she can take it from the let-
terhead."

"So, she calls this number, talks to your people, and
they tell her it's okay," Kimberly said, amazed. Arrang-
ing all of this must have cost Ashlyn a fortune. "Now *I*
don't know what to say."

"Just say 'thank you.' That's easy enough."

"Thank you."

"Now let's get you packed. I'm sure there's a lot you
want to do this weekend. . . ."

Kimberly went to Tanya's house with the other Predators. Tanya's parents were extremely pleasant. They
did anything they could to make the girls feel at home.
No rules seemed to be enforced in Tanya's house. Kimberly soon became convinced that Tanya's parents were
more than a little afraid of their daughter and her
friends.

Tanya's father had a collection of classic cars that he
rarely drove. Tanya told Kimberly that he worshipped
these cars and rarely let *anyone* get their hands on them.
So when he practically jammed the keys to one of the
vehicles in her hand, Kimberly was more than a little
surprised.

She started out for Griff's house, nervous about the
possibility of running into her aunt and uncle, though
she knew it was unlikely given their social calendar.
Neither was in love with the small town life of Cooper
Hollow; when they went out, it was usually to some
event in Manhattan.

Two blocks from Griff's house, Kimberly pulled over.
She sat in the borrowed car for close to half an hour,
thinking. Griff was in terrible trouble and there *was*
something she could do to help him. There would be
consequences for her actions — probably punishment
by her aunt and uncle, definitely punishment by the
authorities at Cooper Riding Academy — but right now,
she didn't care about them.

Kimberly turned the car around and drove down-town to the police station where she and Griff had been taken for questioning. Griff needed an alibi for the time of Rose's murder and she could supply him with one. She knew exactly what she would say:

You see, Detective, he was with me. I snuck out of school that night to be with him. He didn't tell you because he was try-ing to protect me. I'll get kicked out when Ms. Chalmers finds out what I did, but I don't care. Griff is innocent and I can prove it!

It was a lie, but it sounded good. Even if the police broke the alibi later, it would at least direct their atten-tion to finding the real killer. At present, the police were allowing that person to go free. They weren't even *trying* to track the murderer down. Tonight, that would change.

She wanted to tell Griff about her plan, but she knew he would never go along with it. Going to his house now would be the worst thing she could do. He'd be an-gry enough when he found out later on that she'd got-ten herself in trouble in order to help him.

As she pulled into one of the diagonal parking spaces outside the police station, Kimberly also considered that she was about to betray Ashlyn and the other Predators for the sake of a boy. Even if she did not re-veal that they had shown her the way out of Cooper, there would be much tighter security from this point on. The Predators would be trapped in the school and they would never forgive her.

Kimberly frowned. Maybe it was *wrong* to do this after all Ashlyn and Nikki and Tanya had done for her, but she felt as though she had no choice. Griff's *life* was at stake. She would give up anything for him, even the power to run her own life, which her friends seemed to have given her. In a short period of time, he had be-come everything to her. She had never dreamed that she would find a boy who was so confident and gentle, so warm and giving. Her heart had been his the mo-ment he told her about his father the first time they had

106

met. The revelation of feelings had taken such courage.

Shaking herself from her reverie, Kimberly went inside and asked to see the detective in charge of the Gregory Rose homicide. Kimberly was told that Detective Priestly was out but he would return shortly. She quickly found herself back in the waiting area.

Almost an hour passed as Kimberly waited for the detective. Her back ached from sitting so long and after a while she began to pace from one end of the waiting area to the other. One wall had been turned into a mural size bulletin board. She studied the most wanted posters, community service announcements, and public service warnings, then came to the end of the wall, where the faces of missing children peered at her. Kimberly turned away. This was just too depressing.

She tried to walk away from the imploring faces of the missing children, but she felt herself being drawn back to them. Unable to resist the pull of their sad, mournful eyes, Kimberly turned and looked at the posters. Most of the children pictured wore smiles. The photos had been taken for school or at family events. She wondered why their faces had seemed so sad a moment ago. Her eyes must have been playing tricks on her.

Kimberly studied each face carefully. She felt her heart go numb as she thought of the parents who might never know what happened to their children. She thought she could hear the voices of screaming kids being hauled into the backs of unmarked vans. Suddenly, she could stand no more. Before she could look away, however, a single face leaped out of the crowd of photographs.

It was the face of a little girl with curly black hair, braces, and a Cindy Crawford mole beside the crook of her mouth!

Kimberly stumbled back in horror. She had *dreamed* of this child the last time she had been at the precinct house. In her dream, she had given the child to the gray horse. She forced herself to look at the faces of the other children once again. Yes, two more had appeared in her dreams, and had also been taken away by the gray horse. Kimberly was overcome by a mounting fear as she reached up and touched the picture of the girl with the curly black hair.

Reality fell away.

She was racing through the woods, chasing after the gray horse. The little girl on its back was screaming, but she was managing to hold on to the creature's mane. The nightmare horse burst through the edge of the woods and galloped toward the lake. Kimberly screamed for it to stop, but the animal ignored her cries. The gray horse entered the waters, which frothed and sprayed around its powerful legs, and rose up. The child was thrown from its back. The girl landed in the deeper waters, several yards away, and submerged instantly.

Kimberly stood on the shoreline, unable to move. Suddenly, a geyser of thick red blood exploded from the surface of the lake.

Then the waters were still once more.

The dream vanished and Kimberly found herself standing in the lobby of the police station, staring at the poster of the lost child.

Somehow, she kept herself from falling to the floor.

Twenty

The car Tanya's father had loaned to Kimberly started to give her problems shortly after she left the precinct house — without having spoken to Detective Priestly. When she took her foot off the brake the car's speed immediately climbed to fifty-five. She rode the brake and worried that she was going to wear them out before she reached her destination. The car seemed possessed, like a horse that had been spooked and had broken into a frenzied gallop . . .

In a way, Kimberly was grateful for the distraction the faulty brakes provided. *Anything* that would keep her mind off what she had discovered. . . . Then panic seized her. The car might break down before she reached Griff's house.

"Don't even think like that," she chided herself fiercely. "Don't even *think* like that."

She needed Griff desperately. The story she had to tell him was utterly bizarre. She *knew* that she could not expect anyone to believe her, not even Griff. But even if Griff couldn't believe her, she knew that he wouldn't mock her, either. She knew that he would be there for her.

One of two things was happening. Either she was going crazy and the dreams and visions she had been experiencing were signs of her mental deterioration, or the gray horse was real and it was killing little kids — and sometimes bigger ones, like Sharon. Kimberly had only one decent argument for the second possibility: the faces of the missing children. She had seen them *first* in her dreams. If it had been the other way around, if she had seen the faces first on the bulletin board at the police station, then maybe she could accept the simple explanation that she was going insane. But that wasn't the case. This gray horse—this *thing*—was luring kids to their deaths and somehow it had to be *stopped*.

With Griff's help, she might have a chance of defeating the creature from her dreams, the devourer of children, before it consumed another life.

You've been reading too many Nancy Drew mysteries. It doesn't work like that in real life.

Griff's words attacked her thoughts with a stunning ferocity. She managed to forget those words, at least temporarily. Under other circumstances, she might have become angry all over again. Instead, she felt only a slight agitation, like being stuck by the thorns on a rose's stem. You couldn't hate the rose, considering its beauty, but the dull pain from your wound would make it difficult to love the rose exactly the way you had a moment before.

Kimberly reached Griff's house and saw the garage door closed. His red Tempo was not parked outside. Praying that the car was inside the garage, Kimberly drove up the gravel drive, parked, and raced to the front door. Griff's mother appeared after the first knock.

"I heard you driving up," Mrs. Griffiths said. "Car trouble?"

"That's—" Kimberly faltered. That's the least of my problems, she wanted to say, but she knew she could not confide in Mrs. Griffiths. "Is Joel home?"

"I'm sorry, he went out."

Kimberly's heart seized up. If Griff was cruising, he could be out until two in the morning. She needed him now.

"He said he was going to the Night Owl to meet—"

"*Thank you!*" Kimberly said, turning and running back to her car. She knew that she was rude, but she would worry about making apologies later. As she got in her car, she saw Mrs. Griffiths standing in the doorway, watching her. "Thank you, Mrs. Griffiths! Thank you!" she called.

Kimberly pulled out, her car bucking with a sudden burst of acceleration. She slammed on the brake to narrowly avoid colliding with a car that seemed to be out for a leisurely evening drive. Backing into the street, Kimberly tore ahead, passed the car she nearly struck, and raced to the outskirts of town. Soon she was driving through the narrow, winding reaches of Thirteen Bends. Her leg began to ache from the pressure she had to exert to keep the car from accelerating out of control. She could hear the whine of the tortured brakes, but there was nothing she could do about them now.

—too many Nancy Drew mysteries—

Get out of my head! she wanted to scream. Griff will not react like that. He won't turn me off. He'll be kind and understanding. He loves me, damn it, he *loves* me!

Finally, she reached the club. The sight of Griff's red car in the darkened parking lot settled her nerves. She slid into a spot, threw the car in park, killed the lights, then turned off the ignition.

Okay, she told herself, you're here, Griff's here, no one's going anyplace. Try to get yourself under control.

Kimberly sat in the car for almost five minutes, taking deep breaths. She did not want to seem hysterical when Griff saw her. By the time she left the car, her hands had stopped shaking, though she continued to feel slightly ill. Her flesh was clammy, her limbs slightly numb. The taste of iodine was on her tongue. Maybe it was blood from where she had nervously bit her lip.

She went inside and looked around. The jukebox played a love song from that old movie with John Travolta, the one about the mechanical bull. She had danced to this song with Griff.

"May I have this dance," the singer asked passionately, *"for the ressssst of yourrrr liiiiife?"*

Yes, she thought. You can. I love you, Griff.

Kimberly scanned the booths. Griff was not seated at any of them. He was probably in the back, hustling pool or playing video games. She circled the crowd of slow dancing teens and passed through the arched doorway leading to the game room. It was packed, but Griff wasn't there. She turned, decided he was probably in the rest room, and stopped dead. A dozen feet away, a handsome young couple clung to one another. They were dancing cheek to cheek, whispering in each other's ears.

It was Griff. A pretty blond girl was in his arms.

Kimberly's heart shriveled at the sight. This isn't possible, she tried to tell herself. This isn't happening.

The evidence was to the contrary.

Twenty-one

An anger unlike any Kimberly had ever known engulfed her. The murderous rage she had felt toward Gregory Rose the night he had hit her, and toward Sharon Cruise all those times she had harassed her, was *nothing* like what she felt at this moment. As much as she had known pure love for Griff only a few seconds before, she now knew only searing *hatred*.

Kimberly plunged into the crowd of dancers. Seconds before her hand clamped on the hollow between Griff's shoulder and collarbone, she overheard a snatch of his conversation with his new girlfriend. They were talking about her. Probably *laughing* at her!

Griff cried out as Kimberly's hand clawed into his flesh. He was wrenched loose from his dance partner, who stumbled back and fell to the floor.

"Kimberly," Griff said in alarm as he yanked her hand away from his shoulder. "What are you doing?"

"I guess I don't have to ask *you* that."

He looked down to his fallen companion. Two boys were helping her to her feet. "Carolyn, are you—"

"*Talk* to her," Carolyn said with a steady look at Griff. "I'll wait at the booth."

"That's very generous," Kimberly snarled at the girl. "Thanks one whole *hell* of a lot!"

Carolyn ignored Kimberly's words, and quickly vanished into the crowd that had turned its attention on Griff and Kimberly. The blond waitress suddenly appeared.

"Come on, nothing to see," the waitress commanded. "Go back to what you were doing."

Reluctantly, the crowd followed her orders. Those on

113

the dance floor fell back into one another's arms, those at the tables continued to sip their drinks and eat their nachos, those in the back returned to their games. The blond waitress went off to greet a new couple who had just walked in.

Griff pulled Kimberly off to the side of the dance floor, near a vacant booth. "What do you think you're doing? Carolyn could have been hurt."

"She should have been more coordinated."

Griff stared deeply into her face. "Sometimes it's like I don't even know you. What is it, Kimberly? Tell me what's the matter."

She laughed bitterly. Her chest heaved and she felt tears threatening. There was no way she was going to give him the satisfaction of seeing her cry. No way.

"Kimberly—"

"So who's the bimbo?" she asked coldly.

Griff stiffened. "First of all, she's not a bimbo. Second, her name is Carolyn Kohler. We've been friends since we were little kids."

"How sweet."

"Carolyn moved away two years ago," Griff continued. "Her parents are in town and she came with them, to visit. We were catching up. That's *all*."

"Yeah, I could tell. That's why you had your hands all over her."

Griff sighed and stretched his hand toward Kimberly. "There's nothing going *on*, Kimberly," he pleaded. "We're just—"

"You *liar!*" Kimberly roared.

Griff drew back, as if he had been struck. After a moment, he ventured to speak again. "I know what this looks like, but you've *got* to believe me. You know how I feel about you."

"Right now," Kimberly replied acidly, "I don't know anything. I just want to get out of here."

"No," Griff said firmly. "Not until we talk about this. Just sit down with Carolyn and me and we'll straighten everything out. I want us to—"

"All that matters is what *you* want, doesn't it?" Kimberly asked. "Well, that's just great."

"That's not what I meant and you know it."

Kimberly felt her anger growing. It was expanding out of control. Griff had betrayed her. He had been seeing someone else. "I don't think so," she replied through gritted teeth. "I don't think you even want *me*. What you want is a good little girl who'll do whatever you say. Right?"

"No."

"Is that what Carolyn is for you? I guess it's all right with her that you're seeing me. It gives you two something to talk about, something to laugh about behind my *back!*"

Griff shook his head in frustration. "Kimberly," he began, his voice strained, "you're not listening to me. I would have told you I was meeting Carolyn tonight if I could have, but I only found out this morning that she was in town. You were supposed to be at school, and I can't call you there, you know that. What do you want me to do? Apologize? I haven't done anything to apologize about. But if it makes you feel better, fine. I'm sorry."

"You're not sorry. You don't know the meaning of the word. Not yet, anyway."

"Kimberly—"

"I'm going now," she said coldly and started to turn.

"You've got to listen to me!"

Kimberly turned back to face Griff. Her eyes narrowed into slits. "I don't *have* to do anything. You can say anything you want. I don't care. I saw the way you were looking at her. I saw the way you were touching her. I was an *idiot* to think I ever meant anything to you!"

"It's not supposed to be like this," Griff said desperately.

Kimberly laughed. Suddenly, she felt the same way she had felt when she and Ashlyn had been putting Sharon through hell. She felt *powerful* and it was wonderful. She gave herself to her anger and let it shape her next words. "Let me tell you how it's going to be, sweetie. At some point—and I'm not telling you when—I'm going to make

115

a phone call. I'll be distraught, I'll be in tears. You know who I'm going to call?"

Griff swallowed hard. He began visibly to sweat.

"The cops," Kimberly said, ignoring the lure of his sad brown eyes. "I'm going to let them know what happened last week. What *really* happened."

"What are you talking about?" he asked in a hoarse voice, unable to hide his mounting fear.

"I'm going to tell them that I was waiting for you in the woods. Hours went by. You were late. I was getting worried. Then you showed up, all worked up, this crazy look in your eyes. You told me Rose was dead. You killed him."

"That's not what happened," Griff protested, staring at Kimberly in horror. "That's a lie."

Kimberly shrugged. "See ya. Have a nice life. What's left of it." Then she turned and walked away.

Griff chased after her. "Kimberly, you can't do that!"

She laughed at the sound of his frail words. The look of absolute fear she had seen in his gorgeous eyes had *almost* been enough for her. Almost. Maybe she'd have to go through with her threat . . .

Suddenly, Griff's hand was on her shoulder. He was trying to stop her. She turned and before she was even aware of her actions, her hand was moving in a blur, her fingers curled into a fist. The fist connected with something hard. A jarring impact made her jaw shake and pain leapt from her hand up to her shoulders.

Griff stumbled — no, flew — backward into a couple who had been slowdancing. All three went down in a heap. Griff's hand went to his face. Kimberly looked at her clenched fist. There was blood on her knuckles, but it was not her own.

"Good shot," she whispered, staring at her bloody hand. She could never have done anything like this before. She could never have hit someone. Ashlyn had helped her to find power, *real* power. Giddy, Kimberly sauntered toward the door.

She was outside the club, walking to her borrowed car,

when she heard footsteps behind her. "What, do you want some too, little Miss Carolyn?"

"It's not Carolyn."

Kimberly stopped. She recognized the voice. The waitress from the club had followed her outside. Half insane with rage, Kimberly turned to face her. "What do *you* want?"

"I can help you," the waitress said quietly. "You're in over your head. You just don't know it, yet."

"Look, whatever your name is—"

"Jenny."

"Fine. *Jenny.* Everybody's got a place in this world. Yours is waiting tables for minimum wage and whatever tips these kids leave, which probably isn't much. Your place is *not* telling me about my business, so don't even bother trying. Is that clear?"

"You're making a mistake," Jenny said evenly. "Things aren't always what they seem."

Kimberly snorted. "Isn't that profound? First I have to deal with a rich, spoiled bimbo whose number one occupation is harrassing me; then I have to deal with some thrash metal freak whose every other word is stolen from some dead sexist jerk; next I have to put up with a boyfriend who cheats on me; and *now* I've got a waitress following me around with tips on how to live my life. You *know* what you can do with your philosophy, all right?"

Jenny said nothing as Kimberly turned and walked the final few feet to the car. She opened the car door, and was about to climb in when something made her look back to where the waitress had been standing. The young woman was gone. She couldn't have reached the club that fast. Not unless she'd run.

Kimberly pictured the waitress stumbling inside, out of breath, in tears because of what Kimberly had told her. The thought made her smile.

My God, she thought. I sounded exactly like my uncle when I was talking to her. Well, maybe that's not so bad. At least he doesn't take garbage from anyone.

The drive back to Tanya's house was exhilarating.

Kimberly barely slowed the runaway automobile as the sharp turns of Thirteen Bends Road flashed by; the dark shapes of the trees seemed to lean down to snatch at her as she tore past. But she was too fast for them. Her reflexes were razor sharp. She was wired.

Kimberly parked in Tanya's driveway. The car her friend's parents used was gone and the house was dark. Kimberly frowned. She was dying to talk to her friends. She wanted to share all that had happened, wanted to enlist their help in getting back at Griff the way they had gotten back at Sharon, but no one seemed to be home. She tried the front foor and found it unlocked.

The interior of the house was very dark and Kimberly bumped into furniture several times before she found a light switch and flipped it. Nothing. The power must have gone out. She called to her friends, her sense of excitement fading rapidly, replaced by fear.

A noise came from upstairs. Kimberly pictured burglars and knew that she should have fled from the house.

Why should I? she thought insanely. I have *power*. I can handle anything.

Kimberly found the stairs and slowly climbed to the second floor landing. The noise came again. Tanya's bedroom. Something slamming hard against a wall.

Opening the door, Kimberly's heart jumped into her throat. She registered the figure of a man sitting cross-legged in the corner, his back to her. He was crying. Rocking back and forth. Suddenly he lurched forward and slammed his forehead into the wall. He shuddered, then went back to crying and rocking.

The sight terrified Kimberly. It was Tanya's father. He was completely oblivious to her. Images of Tanya, Ashlyn, Nikki, and Tanya's mother lying dead in the basement, hacked to pieces by a madman, exploded in Kimberly's mind. She stumbled back into the corridor, and tried to find the second floor landing. In the darkness, it seemed to have disappeared. The entire corridor had changed somehow. The doorway from which she had just emerged had vanished. There was only one door and

118

it was located at the end of the corridor, near a window.

Break the window and get out, climb out, jump out, whatever, get out of here! a voice in Kimberly's mind screamed.

"You don't have to be afraid," someone whispered from the room at the end of the hall. Kimberly noticed now that the door was slightly ajar. "Everything you want is here. All you have to do is come and take it."

Ashlyn. It was Ashlyn's voice.

Cautiously, Kimberly approached the end of the corridor. Ignoring the window, she pushed the door open and went inside. Ashlyn sat in the darkened room, waiting for her.

"Tanya's dad—" Kimberly began.

"He was bad. He had to be punished. Don't worry about it. Everything's under control."

Kimberly's fears vanished. Vaguely she recalled the missing children and their appearance in her dreams. For some reason, the discovery she had made seemed less urgent than it had earlier. Not exactly her problem. Nevertheless, she told Ashlyn about it now.

When she was through telling her story, Ashlyn only smiled. "I know," she said.

Kimberly was stunned by her friend's calm reaction—and by her answer. Ashlyn couldn't *possibly* know about the missing children. Or about her nightmares.

"We've got to talk," Ashlyn said, drawing near to Kimberly. "It's time."

Kimberly suddenly became aware of the presence of Tanya and Nikki in the room. All three surrounded Kimberly now, moving silently, like shadows.

"Time for what?" Kimberly asked.

Ashlyn smiled. "It's time to see if you can pass the Initiation."

Twenty-two

"The gray horse is real," Ashlyn said. "Most of what you dreamed is real."

Kimberly was surprised that she felt only excitement at this revelation, and shocked that she was so accepting of what could not possibly be the truth. "The gray horse killed Sharon. I saw it."

"No. *You* killed her. The Sentinel attacked her because you wanted him to." Ashlyn shrugged. "If I were you, I wouldn't complain. It's not as if you didn't get something out of the deal."

Kimberly thought of the intellectual ease she had suddenly acquired after Sharon's death. If one killed an enemy, one took on their attributes . . .

"The gray horse is named Sentinel?" Kimberly asked softly. Her head was swimming. *She* had summoned the gray horse? She had controlled it? That couldn't possibly be true. Why then did it feel so *right?*

"No. He is *the* Sentinel. It's both his name and his *duty*. The Sentinel is our protector. He's the guardian of our lord and of all who serve him."

Our lord and all who serve him? Kimberly suddenly felt as if she had been thrown into a bad B-movie.

"Your 'lord?' Who are you talking about?" Kimberly asked. Images of teen cultists raced through her mind.

"He lives in the lake. He has aspects beyond those you can understand. He was old when the world was young."

Kimberly remembered a geyser of blood exploding from the surface of the lake. "A man who lives in the lake? Under the water?"

"Not a man. From before there were men." Ashlyn frowned. "It's complicated. When the time is right, you will meet him. All will be revealed."

120

Kimberly felt her stomach muscles tighten. She was confused. Part of her responded on some deep level to what Ashlyn was telling her, but part of her rejected her friend's zombie-like speech.

As if sensing Kimberly's sudden discomfort, Ashlyn smiled. "I guess we don't have to be so formal about things. The bottom line is that *we* have power and *you* can have it, too. But there's something you have to do to get it. So it all comes down to this: How bad do you want it?"

"What kind of power?" Kimberly asked. From the other room she heard Tanya's father strike his head against the wall once again. She could not help but picture Uncle David in the man's place.

Ashlyn grinned. "Power to do *anything*. Power to *make things happen*. Wanna see?"

"All right," Kimberly said. What else could she say? This was what she had wanted. Even if it was wrong — and she knew deep down that it was — that didn't stop her from wanting it. Images of the day her parents died came to her. She recalled once again the feeling of a stranger holding her back as she tried to race into the burning restaurant. That image was a metaphor for her life. Since that time she had felt frozen, powerless to exert any control over her life. Ashlyn had sensed Kimberly's secret desire for power, for action, and had promised to make it a reality. Kimberly had to hear her out.

Ashlyn turned to a mirror on the wall and gestured at it. Suddenly, their reflections vanished. Kimberly knew that she should have been frightened, but she wasn't. Her curiosity drove her to watch.

Suddenly, another image appeared in the mirror. She saw Ashlyn, Tanya, and Nikki walking through the darkened corridors of Beacon Hall. They went right up to the dorm monitor, made an obscene gesture at the woman, then laughed and kept going. It was as if they were invisible.

"*Yes*," Ashlyn breathed. "That's right. *No one* can see us if we don't want them to."

The scene in the mirror changed. Ashlyn, Tanya, and

Nikki sat in Ashlyn's room, playing a round of the latest Trivial Pursuit game. Surrounding them, books and notebooks flew open of their own accord, and phantom hands caused pens to leap into the air and descend upon the pages. Their work was being done for them.

"That's impossible," Kimberly said, fascinated. "How do you learn anything? How can you pass any tests?"

The image changed once again. Ashlyn was asleep in her bed, a soft white mist breezing through the room. Whispers were born upon those calming winds. The knowledge Ashlyn would need to possess if she were to excel.

"See?" Ashlyn said. "School doesn't have to be such a living hell. Grades and status, getting into an Ivy League College—it can all be done the hard way or the easy way. Your choice."

"Show me more," Kimberly said, thinking of the long, excruciating hours she had spent studying when she could have been enjoying herself.

"Would you like to see how some of the tricks on Sharon were performed?" Ashlyn asked.

"Yeah. Sure," Kimberly said eagerly. The mirror now revealed Sharon sleeping in her room. The notebook on her desk flipped open and the writing on each page suddenly vanished.

"More," Kimberly demanded. The mirror now showed the day in the dining room when Sharon's meal was replaced by the horrible mess she had placed inside Kimberly's little blue bear. The freshman serving the meal was given a proper serving of the day's food. But just before the lid closed over it, the dish magically transformed.

"I want to see more," Kimberly cried. "Show me more!"

"Why don't we give you a taste of how the power can work for you?"

"Yes. Show me." Within the mirror, Kimberly saw the computer room at school. The room was pitch black. Suddenly, one of the machines flared into life. Kimberly's grades were displayed. The low marks suddenly changed, "D"s becoming "B"s.

"I'd make it straight "A"s, but we don't want to get too greedy," Ashlyn said wryly.

Kimberly's mind was racing. She thought of the paper she had gotten back in class the other day. That grade had also changed from a "D" to a "B." She *hadn't* been imagining it. "But the teachers—they'll know these grades were faked!"

"Anything is possible," Nikki said in her sharp, biting voice.

"Anything at all," Tanya added dreamily.

"Do you want to see something *really* scary?" Ashlyn demanded.

"Yeah," Kimberly said.

Suddenly she saw her uncle waking up in the middle of the night. Her aunt, disturbed by the unexpected movement, rolled over, and turned on the light. David Kilpatrick was covered in sweat.

"I wonder if she's okay?" he said.

Who?"

"Kimberly."

"You're kidding me, right?"

"No, really, I think maybe we both came down a little hard on her."

"You must have had a nightmare or something, David. Go back to sleep. Think of a nice corporate merger. Or some old lady squeezed out of her last penny and being put out in the street for one of your housing projects. That usually gives you a good giggle or two."

A look of intense, feral hatred crossed his face. He grabbed her by the tangle of her messy hair and yanked her head back. "I'm telling you, we've got to start treating Kimberly *better*. We're going to start making up for the lousy way we've acted toward her all these years."

"But we've given her—"

"Nothing! Nothing compared to what she needs. We're going to start having her home every weekend and we're going to behave like a *family*." Shaking her head to emphasize each word, he shouted, *"A good loving family!"*

"David—"

"*Is that understood!*" he snarled.

"Yes!" she cried. "Yes, of course, yes!"

A perfectly serene expression settled on his face. "Well. Goodnight, dear."

David lay down again and went directly to sleep while his wife stared at him in open terror. Her chest heaving, she reached for the light switch with trembling fingers and turned it off.

"That's amazing," Kimberly said as the mirror clouded over with black mist. "You could really make that happen?"

"We just did," Ashlyn replied. "The mirror only shows what has already happened, or what's in the process of happening."

"You made that happen," Kimberly said, awestruck.

"No. Our lord made it happen."

Kimberly remembered the forged letter that had given her permission to leave Cooper on the weekends, she remembered the phone call Ms. Chalmers had made. There had been no actors in New York. All of it had been done with Ashlyn's magic.

"But the gray horse, the Sentinel —" As if guided by her words, the mirror suddenly revealed the magnificent gray beast. A small child clung fearfully to its back. It galloped through a clearing, turning at the last moment to stop and turn its blood-red, fiery gaze in Kimberly's direction.

"In return for all our lord gives to us, it needs something in return," Ashlyn said. "It needs the blood of innocents."

"The children," Kimberly said, a sudden horror at the thought of so many dead boys and girls slicing through the deep murk of her thoughts.

Ashlyn seemed confused. "What? The children? No, not the children. That would be a terrible waste, and it would gain our lord nothing at all."

"I don't understand," Kimberly said. "So many children are missing, I saw them in my dreams, I helped give some of them to the Sentinel —"

"Watch," Ashlyn commanded.

Twenty-three

In the mirror, the Sentinel allowed the child to slide from its back. The little dark-haired boy started to run away, but when he saw the gray horse standing perfectly still, he went to the animal and began to stroke its flank. They went off together, deep in the woods.

"The children are like us," Ashlyn said. "They are our lord's hope for the future. No harm comes to them."

"Then why aren't they sent back to their parents?"

"They have to go into the world and spread our lord's influence. They're taken care of, believe me."

"But the parents—"

"The parents of each of these children abused them," Tanya said, breaking in. Her eyes were sharp and alive. "You want them to go back to *that?* Our lord finds decent homes for them. And later, if he needs them, he can call upon them for help."

"What did you think he was doing with the kids?" Nikki asked sourly. "Killing them and eating them?"

"That's sick," Kimberly said. Nevertheless, she could not forget the waking dream she had endured at the police station earlier that night. She had seen the horse throw a child into the water and a geyser of blood explode from the surface of the lake.

"Well, look at what you were thinking," Nikki retorted.

"But you said the blood of innocents, so I just assumed—"

"Never do that," Ashlyn said sharply. "Look, it's really pretty simple. You've been through most of the Initiation so far. In fact, there's only one thing left you have to do. Then you're in."

"What's that?"

"You have to answer a question. I told you this when I first mentioned the Initiation. You said that answering a question was nothing, no problem. And then I told you that you hadn't heard the question. Remember?"

Kimberly nodded.

"So here's the question: Are you willing to pay the price to get what you want out of life?"

"What price?" Kimberly asked in a small voice.

"There's no way to say this so that it doesn't sound corny," Ashlyn said. "But, keep in mind, our lord has been around for thousands of years. Anyway, here it goes. He wants a blood sacrifice to prove your loyalty to him."

"What was Sharon?" Kimberly asked, her throat suddenly dry. In her heart she could no longer deny that she had been responsible for her tormentor's death.

"Practice," Nikki said drily.

"That's enough," Ashlyn said to Nikki. "Kimberly, the sacrifice has to be someone who cares for you, someone you love."

Kimberly's hands gripped each other so tightly that her knuckles turned white. "Griff. I can't."

"What about what you told us when you came in here? That girl he was with. He betrayed you."

"Maybe I overreacted," Kimberly said. "Griff *said* she was only a friend—"

"Grow up," Nikki said.

Ashlyn stepped forward. "No, she's right. Griff was telling the truth. The girl *is* nothing but a friend. Someone he trusts. Someone he can show his *true self* to without fear of rejection."

His true self? Kimberly thought. "What are you saying?"

"Watch," Ashlyn said, gesturing once more at the mirror. In the glass, an image took form. Griff and Carolyn, the girl from the club, sat in the front seat of his car. They had pulled into a deserted parking lot. It looked like an ideal makeout spot, but kissing and petting seemed to be the last thing on Griff's mind.

He was in tears. His chest heaved and he blubbered like

126

a baby. Kimberly felt instant revulsion at the sight. The girl beside Griff took him in her arms and urged him to get it all out. She promised that everything would be all right. Kimberly suddenly wished that she could reach through the mirror and tell her exactly how wrong she was.

"The moment I saw her I wanted her in my life," Griff said, his nose running, his words coming out as if he had a terrible cold. "I wanted her so much that I was willing to be whatever she needed me to be. I tried to create this, I dunno, this image of myself as very open. I was nervous so I just started talking. I'm like — I was such an idiot. I told her everything. All the stuff about my dad. Even stuff that wasn't true. Anything I could think of that would make me seem, um, y'know, vulnerable."

"That's fine, sweetie," the girl said as she stroked his hair. "Let it out."

"I wanted to just be myself, but I knew I wouldn't be good enough for her."

"Don't say that, Joel."

"It's true. Friday night, I almost didn't show up at all for our date. I was so sure she wasn't going to be there, that I was imagining it all, that I almost just stayed home with my mom. I was just going to sit there and listen to my tapes. They couldn't hurt me. Not like she could."

"Maybe you should have," the girl said.

"No," Griff said. "I'm glad for every minute I had with her. I know I'll never get her back, but I'd do anything, anything at all, just so that she wouldn't be mad at me? I just kept wanting to ask her, 'are you mad at me?' Even when she was smiling at me, I couldn't trust what I was seeing."

Kimberly did not believe what she was hearing. Griff was running himself down for the very traits that had made Kimberly fall in love with him in the first place. She loved his strength, his openness, and his willingness to accept that he needed someone in his life. In the mirror, Griff was claiming to be the opposite of everything she had loved about him.

"You've got more important concerns," the girl said. "What about the police?"

"God," he whispered. "I didn't kill Gregory Rose. You've got to believe me. I never even had the guts to get into a real fight with that creep. I always backed down.

"Now I'm going to spend my whole life in jail. They don't have any other real suspects. I know they don't. They're going to try me, convict me, and sentence me to life for something I didn't do. Oh, God!"

Kimberly couldn't believe this display. Griff was falling to pieces. He had looked into her eyes and had told her that *she* was turning into someone else. What a hypocrite! At least she had had the guts to be honest with him. He had been a complete coward all along.

"I've got to run," Griff said. "It's my only chance."

"That's as good as admitting your guilt."

"I don't care!" he cried. "I'm not going to jail. I've got to get out of here. Go somewhere and hide."

The girl nodded. "I can help you. I've got some money saved up. I'll find a way to get it to you."

"Thank you," he whimpered. "Thank you."

"I don't want to see any more of this!" Kimberly screamed as she threw a punch at the mirror. Ashlyn caught her hand before she could make contact.

"He loves you," Ashlyn said.

"I can't believe I didn't see him for what he is!"

"And what's that?"

"Weak. A joke."

"But he *loves* you," Nikki taunted.

Ashlyn drew Kimberly close and gently touched the side of her face. "You can have everything you've ever wanted. But there's a price. You have to part with the old. Give Griff to us. Will you pay our price?"

Kimberly hesitated. Earlier tonight, when she had decided to go to the police and give Griff an alibi, she had

128

**HOW TO APPLY
YOUR TATTOO:**
1. Moisten the area you want tattooed with water (not too wet or the ink will smear, not too dry, or it won't stick).
2. Place tattoo face down and press on slightly moistened area for a few seconds.
3. Lift up, and now you are tattooed.
4. Washes off with soap and water.
NOTE: Although the tattoo is printed using safe, non-toxic vegetable FDA regulated colors, they are not recommended for sensitive skin or near eyes or to be taken internally.

**HOW TO APPLY
YOUR TATTOO:**
1. Moisten the area you want tattooed with water (not too wet or the ink will smear, not too dry, or it won't stick).
2. Place tattoo face down and press on slightly moistened area for a few seconds.
3. Lift up, and now you are tattooed.
4. Washes off with soap and water.
NOTE: Although the tattoo is printed using safe, non-toxic vegetable FDA regulated colors, they are not recommended for sensitive skin or near eyes or to be taken internally.

**HOW TO APPLY
YOUR TATTOO:**
1. Moisten the area you want tattooed with water (not too wet or the ink will smear, not too dry, or it won't stick).
2. Place tattoo face down and press on slightly moistened area for a few seconds.
3. Lift up, and now you are tattooed.
4. Washes off with soap and water.
NOTE: Although the tattoo is printed using safe, non-toxic vegetable FDA regulated colors, they are not recommended for sensitive skin or near eyes or to be taken internally.

**HOW TO APPLY
YOUR TATTOO:**
1. Moisten the area you want tattooed with water (not too wet or the ink will smear, not too dry, or it won't stick).
2. Place tattoo face down and press on slightly moistened area for a few seconds.
3. Lift up, and now you are tattooed.
4. Washes off with soap and water.
NOTE: Although the tattoo is printed using safe, non-toxic vegetable FDA regulated colors, they are not recommended for sensitive skin or near eyes or to be taken internally.

**HOW TO APPLY
YOUR TATTOO:**
1. Moisten the area you want tattooed with water (not too wet or the ink will smear, not too dry, or it won't stick).
2. Place tattoo face down and press on slightly moistened area for a few seconds.
3. Lift up, and now you are tattooed.
4. Washes off with soap and water.
NOTE: Although the tattoo is printed using safe, non-toxic vegetable FDA regulated colors, they are not recommended for sensitive skin or near eyes or to be taken internally.

**HOW TO APPLY
YOUR TATTOO:**
1. Moisten the area you want tattooed with water (not too wet or the ink will smear, not too dry, or it won't stick).
2. Place tattoo face down and press on slightly moistened area for a few seconds.
3. Lift up, and now you are tattooed.
4. Washes off with soap and water.
NOTE: Although the tattoo is printed using safe, non-toxic vegetable FDA regulated colors, they are not recommended for sensitive skin or near eyes or to be taken internally.

been willing to sacrifice herself and to betray her friends for Griff. She had loved him that much. But first in the club, and then in the mirror, Griff had shown her that he didn't deserve her love. Ashlyn was right. All he deserved was the same thing Gregory Rose had gotten.

"You killed Gregory Rose, didn't you?" Kimberly asked.

"The Sentinel acted on my desires," Ashlyn said, "the same as he did for you with Sharon. He lives to protect us."

"All I have to do is give Griff to you?"

"Yes," Ashlyn said.

"Then I can do what you can do? I can have anything I want, any time I want it?"

"Yes. Power without limits."

Kimberly shook her head. It just didn't seem like a fair trade. Kimberly couldn't believe that was all there was to the deal. Ashlyn's "lord" would certainly want more from them, just as it would want something more from the children it was helping. Wouldn't it? But, for now, in her pain and her anger, Kimberly was willing to ignore that eventuality. She had endured too much agony in the past. It was time to start getting what she wanted out of life. For that, she was willing to pay *any* price.

"You've already had a taste of that power," Ashlyn said. "Remember at the club tonight? We were watching you; we were with you. Well, now I'm going to give you another taste of the power we're offering. Think about what you want most in life, what you've always dreamed of having. Think about it and it can be made a reality."

"Right here and now?"

"Yes."

"It sounds like you want me to make a wish."

"Why don't you?"

You can't, a voice whispered deep within Kimberly, because if you tell anyone your wish, it won't come true.

As if sensing her thoughts, Ashlyn said, "I'll leave you alone with the mirror. You should have some privacy."

Ashlyn, Tanya and Nikki left the room. Kimberly waited until she heard the door shut behind them before she thought about her heart's desire. An image formed in the mirror. Kimberly saw two faces take shape and nearly wept as she recognized the images of her real mother and father. They looked the same as they had in the only surviving photograph Kimberly owned. She began to cry.

"We love you, Kimberly," the faces in the mirror said.
"I'm so sorry," Kimberly sobbed.
"You mustn't be. What happened wasn't your fault. We're very, very proud of the woman you've become."

Kimberly reached into the cold regions whose borders had been the edges of the mirror. She knew that her fingers should only be touching the mirror's hard surface, but, impossibly, they went through the surface, into the darkness beyond. Her mother stretched out her hand to Kimberly. Their fingers touched briefly, then the image flickered and faded. Kimberly drew out her hands, suddenly afraid of what else she might touch in the mirror's dark realm.

She wept openly Ashlyn came to get her.

Twenty-four

Kimberly was still shaking later that night as she and Ashlyn sat alone in the living room. Some semblance of order had been restored to Tanya's house. The electricity was back on, the house no longer appeared to contain any strange passages, and even Tanya's father was back to normal. Tanya's mother had returned shortly after Ashlyn led Kimberly out of the darkened room with the mirror, into the well-lit corridor. She had been out grocery shopping for all of Kimberly's favorite foods. Kimberly knew she hadn't made any special requests, but, at this point, she was beyond questioning such a minor unusual occurrence.

"You can do anything. You can *fix* anything, right?" Kimberly asked as they watched an episode of a T.V. program that had been on when Kimberly was very young. Ashlyn had been able to make the episodes appear at will.

Ashlyn nodded. "Anything at all. You will, too, if you truly become one of us."

"I don't want Griff getting away from me," Kimberly said vehemently. "Have someone else confess to the murder. I don't care who. We can clear them later."

"That's fine," Ashlyn said. "Is that your answer? Will you pay our price?"

"Yes," Kimberly said darkly. "I will."

"Good," Ashlyn said with a delicious smile. "Kimberly, you've made the right decision. You're one of us now. *A Predator.*"

Kimberly didn't need the magic mirror to know that her smile perfectly matched Ashlyn's.

That night, however, Kimberly was unable to sleep. As she lay in the dark, she found her excitement giving way to anxiety. She spent the entire night staring at the ceiling, replaying every word of her earlier conversations with Ashlyn.

By morning, her decision to become a Predator was no longer as firm as it had been the night before. Then, Kimberly had been caught up in the ecstasy of Ashlyn's promise—that she could have her heart's deepest desire fulfilled. And that desire *had* been fulfilled, her dearest wish granted before her very eyes. She had seen her parents again—had almost been able to touch them. She had spoken to them and they had told her that they were proud of her.

For a brief time afterward, Kimberly had felt reborn, like a new person, like an explorer who had just discovered a fantastic world existing side by side with the only one she had ever known. She had been filled with a breathless enthusiasm.

But later, in bed, as she watched the night shadows play across the walls and ceiling, her euphoria had waned. In its stead came reason—and the memory of love. Kimberly had thought of Griff, of how much he had meant to her, and then of what she had promised to do to him. How could her parents possibly be proud of a daughter who was preparing to sacrifice her boyfriend to some *thing* so that she could be in control of her life? It was crazy.

For most of the day, Kimberly shied away from close conversation with Ashlyn and the others. Late Saturday afternoon, however, Tanya approached her.

"I know what you're going through," she said to Kimberly. "It's hard. I was the last one to be made a Predator before you. There's a—I dunno—a period of adjustment you have to go through. But once you *do* it, once the Initiation is all over with, you'll feel fine. You won't worry any more. The things that seem important to you right now won't matter at all. I'm happier now than I've ever been."

Upstairs, the thumping had begun again. This time, it was Tanya's mother who had been "bad" and was being punished. Tanya gave a little giggle at the sound of her mother thumping her own head against the wall, wailing in torment.

"Just get through this thing with Griff and you'll see that I'm right. Everything will be much better for you."

Tanya's words did little to reassure Kimberly or to appease her growing sense of guilt. Still, she gave Tanya what she hoped could be read as a smile of gratitude and then asked to borrow her father's car again. Tanya's warm expression cooled suddenly.

"Where do you want to go?"

"I don't know," Kimberly said with a shrug that was perhaps too casual. "Out."

Tanya's smile returned. "Why don't I come with you?"

Kimberly swallowed hard. "Oh, that's all right. Actually, I might just lay down for awhile instead."

"Sure," Tanya said. "Sleep as long as you like."

Kimberly went upstairs and into the guest room she had been given. Wearily, she lay upon the bed. The banging continued. Again she wondered what she had agreed to by sacrificing Griff—when suddenly, images of Griff's betrayal leaped into her mind. Anger suffused her. She pictured Griff's head being driven into the wall. Uncle David's. Aunt Margaret's. Sharon's. Gregory Rose's.

Damn them all. It was worth it. Any price was worth it to get back at them.

Kimberly clutched her head. No, that was wrong! She couldn't allow herself to think that way! Where were these violent thoughts and impulses coming from!

The banging ceased. Kimberly heard raised voices. Tanya and Ashlyn arguing. A soft knock came at Kimberly's door. The door opened and Tanya's mother peeked inside.

"I hope I didn't disturb you, Kimberly," she said in a "sitcom mom" voice. "I was just putting up a picture in one of the guest bedrooms."

"No problem," Kimberly replied softly.

Tanya's mother smiled lovingly. "You just try to get some sleep now. You look tired."

"I am."

The door shut and Kimberly closed her eyes. She slept without dreams and when she woke it was still sunny out.

But how could that be? Her limbs were stiff and there was a kink in her neck. Kimberly looked at the clock on the nightstand and saw that it was after ten—in the morning. She had slept through the night. Clearly, she had needed the rest more than she had known.

Kimberly went downstairs, afraid of what she might see in the faces of her friends. Anger? Condemnation? Instead, she found Ashlyn, Tanya, and Nikki in the den playing a game of Monopoly, with warm, inviting smiles on their faces. The four girls spent the day together, playing board games, driving around town, and even taking in a movie. Absolutely no mention was made of the Initiation and there were no repeats of the previous day's bizarre events. Kimberly once again felt the urge to be alone, but Ashlyn and the others subtly discouraged her. By the time the four girls were driven back to Cooper by Tanya's parents, Kimberly was exhausted. She wondered if the whole weekend had been nothing more than a horrible nightmare. The disturbing revelation at the police station; Griff's betrayal with Carolyn; the mirror of dreams.

Kimberly lay on her bed in Beacon Hall and tried to put the events of the weekend out of her mind. But she could not forget the feel of her mother's hand as it briefly touched hers and she *knew* that the experience had been *real*. All of it. Before long she fell into a deep sleep that was invaded by a nightmare of the gray horse—the Sentinel. In the dream, the Sentinel tossed children into the black lake; its waters ran bright red, even in the moonlight. Kimberly's parents stood on the shore of the lake, smiling in approval as the children were consumed.

Kimberly woke abruptly at four in the morning and was afraid to go back to sleep. If everything Ashlyn had told her about the Sentinel and the lord it served was true, that it was good to the children and to the girls, why was she having these terrible nightmares? Ashlyn had sworn that the children were not harmed and that they were being rescued from abusive homes. But somehow if she were honest with herself, the idea of some ancient creature that lived in a lake acting as a social worker did not ring true.

134

Not even a little bit. Kimberly had been so out of her mind with irrational anger the other night, she had been willing to believe *anything* Ashlyn told her.

The next day, after one of their classes, Kimberly took Ashlyn aside and said, "I still don't understand. What is it we *do* for this, y'know this *thing?* I mean, it's giving us the world, and it doesn't seem to want much in return."

"Does it matter?" Ashlyn asked. For what our lord give to us, I'd do anything it asked. And I wouldn't bother to ask unnecessary questions."

Kimberly nodded. "There's something else," she said, braving Ashlyn's slightly cold look. "Tanya said that you lost your parents, too."

Ashlyn stiffened. "She shouldn't have."

"Is it true?"

"Yes. They died in a plane crash two years ago."

"I'm sorry," Kimberly said simply as she lightly touched Ashlyn's arm. Ashlyn covered Kimberly's fingers and squeezed.

"My parents were wonderful. The best a girl could have wanted, y'know?"

Kimberly nodded. "How did you end up here?"

"My mom and dad were rich. No surviving relatives. They had a corporation. I inherit everything, but not until I'm twenty-one. Until then, the company takes care of me. The new CEO and his wife were appointed conservator and they thought it best to send me here. End of story."

"I didn't know."

"Now you do."

"You miss them?"

"Sometimes."

"Do you wonder what they would think of what we're doing?"

A cross expression appeared on Ashlyn's face at the sound of Kimberly's question. "All we're doing is taking care of ourselves. They're not here to do it. If they *were* here right now, none of this would be happening."

Kimberly blanched. It sounded as if Ashlyn was angry at her parents for dying, for deserting her. For years, Kim-

135

berly had been so consumed by guilt over her parents' death that being *angry* with them for abandoning her had never even occurred to her.

"Yeah, maybe you're right," Kimberly said slowly.

"You know it." Ashlyn looked around. "You're calling Griff tonight."

"Tonight?"

"Yes."

"We're doing it tonight?"

"No. Friday. Everything's set for Friday."

The bell rang.

Ashlyn frowned. "I'll be late for class. See ya!"

Kimberly waved feebly as Ashlyn ran off. Friday night. Griff would die on Friday night. Once again, she would be responsible for the death of someone she loved. Kimberly raised a hand to her forehead.

It felt hot. The image of Griff she'd glimpsed in the magic mirror came back to her. She didn't love *him*, that boy she'd seen in the glass. She had loved the *lie* he had created in order to win her.

She hated him for that.

But was hate a good enough reason for committing murder? If on the very night Kimberly had learned the truth about Griff, Ashlyn had proposed they go out and serve Griff up to whatever strange lake creature the girls worshipped, Kimberly in the heat of new anger, might have jumped at the chance. But time had caused her anger to chill and her reason to return. She was still angry with Griff, yes. And she did, indeed, hate him. But enough to *kill* him? Enough to kill *anyone?*

She was no longer certain. And where could she turn for advice?

Ashlyn had claimed that Sharon was dead because of the force of her desire. Kimberly couldn't deny that there had been many times when she had wanted Sharon out of her life, when she may even have wished to kill Sharon herseslf. But there was an important distinction between *wanting* to do something and actually *doing* it. She could fantasize all she wanted about Sharon being tied to a chair while she approached with a straight razor. That didn't mean she actually wanted to *touch* Sharon with a straight razor.

And then, Kimberly felt the phantom touch of her mother's hand brushing against hers. The sensation stilled her frantic thoughts. The reality was that she could have her parents back. The thing in the lake could do that for her. It could do anything.

God help her, she wanted it so badly. She missed her parents so much. Needed them so desperately.

Enough to pay any price, she realized. Any price at all.

Twenty-five

Kimberly made the call to Griff that night. She told him that she had been out of her mind with jealousy the night she had seen him with Carolyn, and that once she had had a chance to calm down and think rationally about Griff's explanation, she knew that she had been overreacting. And besides, the deaths of Gregory Rose and Sharon Cruise had rattled her . . .

"I love you," Griff said when Kimberly had finished speaking.

"You, too," she said uneasily. Kimberly hung up the phone. Ashlyn and the other Predators sat next to her on Mrs. Alcott's bed. The magic wielded by the girls had been used to send the older woman on an errand for the next hour.

Nikki and Tanya collapsed on the bed, giggling and making "kissy-face" motions. Ashlyn stared at Kimberly with a dark and knowing smile.

"You're doing good," Ashlyn said. "How do you feel about the big night?"

Kimberly thought of the image in the mirror, the image of her parents. "Wonderful," she said simply.

It was worth it, she told herself, it *had* to be worth it. Griff had betrayed her. He did not deserve her loyalty. Ashlyn and the other Predators had saved her from torment at Sharon's hands, they had opened her up to power beyond reason. They were her friends. No harm would come to her so long as she trusted them.

Later that evening, Kimberly returned to her room and tried to sleep, but the nightmares came with immediate and startling ferocity. In one of them, she stood by as her parents laughed with insane, hyena laughs, and forced little children upon the gray horse. They encouraged Kimberly to do the same and when she refused, they chased

138

after her, their eyes burning with the same blood-red fire she had seen in the eyes of the Sentinel.

Kimberly awakened abruptly. Something about her parents' dream appearance troubled her. She got out of bed and went to the lone picture she had of them, their engagement photo, and scrutinized it carefully. Her dream parents looked exactly the way they did in this photograph, down to their clothing. Young and beautiful. Nothing was wrong.

Everything was wrong.

But *what* was it that was wrong about her parents' dream appearance? It was, after all, not only the way they looked in the engagement photograph but also the way they had appeared in Ashlyn's magic mirror. Why hadn't she been troubled before this? And *what* was it, exactly, that was troubling her?

And why still the nightmares at this point? she wondered, nervously pacing her room. Ashlyn had known about her dreams. Did she also know about these nightmares? Could Kimberly risk telling her?

There was no risk, she chided herself. She was trusting Ashlyn with her life, with her soul even. No secrets should exist between them. Kimberly threw on a robe and left her room. She slipped past Mrs. Alcott's open door and went to the wing in which the other Predators lived.

Ashlyn's door was locked. Kimberly tapped at it for a moment, then turned away. It was clear. The Predators had gone out and they had not invited her. Kimberly felt flush. She turned and tried to wrench the door off its hinges. She had to know if Ashlyn was in there, ignoring her, or if her fears of having been left behind were correct. She couldn't budge the door. The brief surge of unnatural strength she had experienced at the club did not repeat itself.

A ragged breath escaped her. She had not yet been given the power to open locks with a thought. She turned away, disappointed, then heard a strange sound. When she looked back, she caught a glimpse of a luminescent figure in a white dress rounding the corner at the end of the hall.

Beside her, she heard a click. Turning sharply, she saw Ashlyn's door open. Kimberly went inside. Ashlyn was gone.

Damn her!

She was being excluded again. Well, maybe that was to be expected. She wasn't a Predator yet. There was still the last phase of the Initiation. Then all the remaining secrets would be revealed, or so she had been led to believe.

Kimberly was curious. She began to look around the room. She didn't know what she hoped to find, only that she wanted some real answers before she agreed to a lifetime commitment. A light flickered behind her, causing her own shadow to rise up before her. Kimberly spun around, her heart ready to explode, and saw the edge of something poking out from beneath Ashlyn's pillows. A book of some kind. Strange that she hadn't seen it before.

The light had already vanished. Kimberly sat on the bed and used a penlight from Ashlyn's desk to examine the book. Its cover was dirty brown but pretty sturdy; its pages were crisp and yellowed. She opened the book carefully and was immediately and keenly disappointed. The book seemed to be a diary of some kind, but it was written in a language Kimberly could not decipher.

Kimberly's logical side told her that the book couldn't be all that important. If it was, why had Ashlyn left it out in the open, where it could so easily be found? Still, she decided to take the journal back to her room. Maybe the strange writing was some ancient language, the language of the ancient lake creature. Maybe the creature, the girls' lord, had written the book; maybe the secrets for controlling it were scrawled somewhere in its pages. All Kimberly had to do was to figure out what language the book was written in and then find someone who could read it.

That meant betraying her friends.

But maybe not. Kimberly needed answers and her friends were holding back. As Ashlyn said, who could object to their taking care of themselves? After all, wasn't that the real difference between a predator and its prey? One had power, the other didn't. Rather than view her act as a betrayal of the group, they should judge it as the act of a true Predator.

Kimberly hurried back to her room and changed into her casual clothes. Then she carefully wrote down one passage of the book. After that, she left the school grounds for the woods where she buried the diary in a deep hole.

Kimberly expected Ashlyn to miss the journal, but on Tuesday she made no mention of its being gone. Kimberly made casual inquiries to several of the language teachers at the school, but none of them recognized the language of the passage. Over the course of the week, Kimberly considered digging up the book and finding a way to return it to Ashlyn, but she never seemed to find the chance.

The dreams of the gray horse, the devourer of children, had become unbearable.

In one, her parents had melted together and transformed into a hideous representation of the Sentinel. The figure in the luminescent dress was there too, the one she had glimpsed in the hallway outside Ashlyn's room, the one she had glimpsed in the woods the night she had first met Griff, staring mournfully at Kimberly as the night's horror unfolded. Kimberly wanted the dreams to stop, but she had been unable to bring herself to tell Ashlyn about them.

Ashlyn had sworn that the creature in the lake was not murdering the children brought to it by the Sentinel, but to Kimberly, no other explanation made sense. If indeed that turned out to be the case, that the Sentinel was acting as a courier of death, could she live with such knowledge? The *others* had been able to go on in possession of such knowledge. True, Tanya had spoken of a period of adjustment.

Kimberly decided to wait and see. If she were to find *proof* that the creature was killing the children it claimed to be helping, then she would do something about it — even if she was already a Predator.

It wasn't until Friday night, on the way to her final meeting with Griff, that Kimberly had time to stop and dig up the journal. She had decided that she would wait until the

Initiation was complete to return it to Ashlyn. There would be no way for Ashlyn or the others to punish her once they were equals — or so she hoped.

The memory of her last nightmare returned to Kimberly as she walked alone through the blackened woods. Her parents — something was wrong with the way they looked. She had felt this again. But *what* was wrong?

Ahead, Kimberly saw Griff's car. She had asked him to meet her where he had picked her up, the night she had first joined the Predators and the night Gregory Rose had struck her.

Kimberly stopped and removed the photograph of her parents from her jeans. She had to figure this out, now. What could be *wrong* with the way her parents looked in the mirror and in her dreams? They looked exactly the same as they looked in the engagement photograph she held in her hand . . .

Then it came to her. The revelation struck her with unbearable force, nearly bringing her to her knees.

It was a lie. Everything Ashlyn had told her was a lie!

She stared at the photograph and looked at her father's full, wavy hair and her mother's full, youthful figure. This wasn't the way they had looked when they had died in the restaurant. By that time they had been married for twelve years. Her father's hair had thinned and her mother's figure had never fully recovered from her pregnancy. The clothes they had worn when the photograph was taken had been thrown out long before the time they died.

The images in the mirror were false. They had been created on the basis of the only photograph Kimberly had of her parents. Suddenly she remembered something she had read about con artists posing as psychics. The victim of such deceptions was told to close his eyes while the "spiritual advisor" attempted to contact a loved one. While the victim's eyes were closed, the con man picked the pockets of his prey and based his "amazing glimpses" into his victim's life upon the information he had gathered from the contents of the person's wallet.

Kimberly's parents had *not* come back to her. They had

142

not spoken to her. It had been Ashlyn's "lord" who had spoken to her. She should have seen the deception from the start, but the truth was that she had wanted to believe the lie so *badly,* and Ashlyn and her friends had expertly preyed upon Kimberly's head.

How could her parents possibly be proud of the young woman she'd become? How could she have believed her parents to say that? She had acted monstrously. But maybe it wasn't too late.

Suddenly Kimberly *knew* that many of the other "revelations" she had seen in the magic mirror were no more than lies. The children she had seen and dreamt of were brutally murdered, not led to a bright future. Her uncle's sudden reversal in attitude had no basis in fact. And Griff—his confession to Carolyn had been fabricated by Ashlyn. Griff was always who he had presented himself to be. It was all Ashlyn's doing. She had been willing to do whatever it took, tell her whatever she wanted to hear, distort reality to whatever extent she could, just to bring her around.

Kimberly made her decision. Ashlyn had lied to her. She had used her. If Kimberly were to complete the Initiation, she would be prey once again, *not* predator. The weight of the book in the waistband of her jeans comforted her. It was a weapon she could use against the others. It had to be. She *had* to save the children they were murdering. At least, she had to try.

Now the only question was whether she would fight Ashlyn and the others alone. Kimberly wanted to run into Griff's waiting arms, but she had to know something first. Ashlyn had lied about her parents and about her uncle. No doubt she had lied about Griff, too. Still, no one had ever meant as much to Kimberly as Griff did; it wouldn't hurt, she reasoned, to go cautiously with him, to see for herself just how true he was to her. If she sensed a reluctance on his part to accept her again, or if she felt just one grain of duplicity in him, she would leave and face the Sentinel alone.

Was Griff with her? Kimberly walked forward, determined to find out.

Twenty-six

Griff had been unable to sleep for days. Kimberly's explosion at the club the previous Saturday night haunted him even more than his fears of going to jail for the murder of Gregory Rose. At least those worries had been dispelled by the unexpected confession of Tommy Bryant, one of Rose's band members. The business with Kimberly still troubled him.

He sat behind the wheel of his Tempo, parked in the exact spot he had first seen Kimberly on one of the roads winding through the woods. It was nearly as late as it had been that night, too.

His thoughts went back to Saturday night. Something dark and alien had burned in Kimberly's eyes. She had truly loathed him and wanted to hurt him. Her final words — her threat to go to the police and lie about his involvement in Rose's murder — had caused him to be genuinely afraid of what she might do. The Kimberly he had first met, the one with whom he had fallen in love, had not been the Kimberly who had threatened him. Something else had taken her place.

Later that night, he had spoken to his mother about Kimberly's strange behavior. She told him about the first time *she* had fallen in love. She told him about the feelings being overwhelming. She told him that she had spent days locked in her room crying, or floating around in a joyous haze, oblivious to her parents, to her problems, to everything but the sound of her boyfriend's voice. To this day, his mother told him, she missed that boy she first loved. The discussion helped Griff be tolerant when, early in the week, Kimberly called to arrange their date tonight.

Griff thought that on the phone Kimberly had sounded

wounded and frightened. The stark, feral hatred she had displayed that last Saturday night had disappeared from her tone. She had told him that she loved him and that she needed him. Nothing else mattered to Griff. Meeting Kimberly had made him happier than he had ever been. He prayed that tonight, everything would go back to normal between them.

Griff was about to put on a tape of an old time radio program when a light tapping came from window beside his head. A rush of absolute rapture moved through him as he twisted in his seat and saw Kimberly peering in through the window with a warm, loving smile on her beautiful face. She stood back so that Griff could open the door. He left the car and threw himself into her waiting arms, not even bothering to close the door behind him. The relentless *dinging* tone that indicated an open door while the key was in the ignition became maddening after a few seconds. Kimberly allowed one of her hands to stop roaming the contours of Griff's sturdy back and shove the door closed.

"Thank you," he whispered.

Despite her being in his arms, Griff sensed a stiffness in Kimberly's motions, a hesitancy he wanted desperately to overlook, but could not. Whatever had been troubling her on Saturday night had not gone completely away. He held her for a few moments more, then kissed her. She responded passionately, but her lips were cold. Griff pulled back.

"Tell me what's wrong," he urged. He knew that the pressures of school were getting to her; he knew that her aunt and uncle were less than sympathetic figures; he knew that the deaths of Gregory Rose and Sharon Cruise had to be having some effect on her; and he knew that he'd unintentionally hurt her by going out with Carolyn last Saturday night. Poor Kimberly, he thought.

"It's nothing," she whispered.

"You're shaking."

"No, I'm fine," she protested.

Griff stared into her eyes and saw an incredible conflict

145

raging there.

"I've got something for you," she whispered, her chest rising and falling dramatically.

"You do?" he asked. She nodded and looked toward the trail that led back to Cooper Riding Academy. Shuddering, she bit her lip and fixed him with a sharp, desperate stare.

"I want you to tell me something," she said. "Tell me the absolute truth. I'll *know* if you're lying."

"All right."

"What went on between you and that girl at the club Saturday night after I left?"

"Nothing."

"You didn't drive her home?"

"No," Griff answered simply. "Alan Peyton met us there. I don't think I ever mentioned Alan to you. He's a cool guy. You'd like him. Anyway, he got there about five minutes after you left. Alan and Carolyn have had this on-again, off-again thing for years. I left the club about ten minutes after he arrived. When Alan and Carolyn get started, neither of them knows anyone else is around. Besides, you—well, I was pretty upset. I needed to be on my own."

Kimberly did not look away from his kind and trusting face. Suddenly, tears welled up in her eyes. Just as she had hoped. The images in the mirror had been a lie. Griff had not betrayed her after all.

"Kimberly?"

"We have to get back in the car," she said, grabbing hold of his arm. Her eyes flickered nervously to the opening in the woods.

"Why? I thought you had a surprise for me."

"Just trust me," Kimberly said, looking around as if she heard something coming. "We've got to do it *now.*"

Griff got behind the wheel as Kimberly ran around the car and jumped into the passenger side.

"Roll up the windows. Lock the doors," Kimberly commanded, already in the process of doing as much on her side of the car.

Griff chose not to argue or question.

"Good," she said. "Now get us out of here."

"Where do you want to go?"

"I dunno. Go into town, I guess. I can't go back to Cooper. Not tonight."

Nodding, Griff made a narrow U-turn and headed toward his house.

They did not speak for a few moments. Kimberly was sweating, despite the chill in the air. She had done it. The decision was made. Ashlyn's "lord" would be cheated out of its prey. Now all she had to do was stay alive.

They were heading into town when Kimberly told Griff about the gray horse, the dreams, Ashlyn, Gregory Rose, and Sharon. She could tell from his expression that he wanted desperately to believe her, but she knew the story was too fantastic. How could anyone believe it to be true unless he had lived through it?

"Kimberly, you know I'll help you in any way I can, but—"

With an involuntary shudder, Griff reached for his signal flasher and pulled it back once, to turn on his brights.

Directly ahead, standing in the middle of the road, were Ashlyn, Tanya, and Nikki. Behind them was the gray horse, its eyes bright crimson.

Griff's car was barreling forward at sixty miles an hour. He jammed on the brakes, but Kimberly knew the car wouldn't stop in time to avoid a collision.

Twenty-seven

Griff was about to cut the wheel sharply to the left when Kimberly with a display of incredible strength, grasped it with both hands and held it firm. The headlights washed over the figures rising up before them and Kimberly was certain that Ashlyn frowned instants before impact.

But there was no impact. His Tempo passed directly through the figures gathered in the road. They had not been real. The figures were an illusion.

"They wanted us to crash," Kimberly explained. "Ashlyn figured you'd spin off the road, into the trees."

Griff looked at her, eyes wide, heart pounding.

"Keep your eyes on the *road!*" Kimberly commanded.

Nodding, Griff followed her order.

A glance in the rear view mirror revealed two burning red lights. Kimberly wanted to believe it was a car of some kind. A motorcycle. Anything. But she was unable to train her thoughts away from the glowing crimson eyes of the horse.

"They're still coming," Kimberly whispered.

A tapping came from the direction of Kimberly's passenger side window. Both Kimberly and Griff turned their heads sharply to the right. Then, from the other side of the car, a hideous voice erupted. "Boo!"

A hand crashed through the driver's side window. Shards of glass sliced across Griff's face and throat. Before Griff could move in his own defense, the hand fastened on his neck. His hands sprung from the steering wheel and he tried to claw the inhumanly strong hand away. The car was going out of control when Kimberly caught the steering wheel once more.

Kimberly used one hand to guide the car through the twisting road as the other grasped at the hand on Griff's

148

neck. Even before she saw the grinning face of the crazed auburn-haired girl hanging on outside the car, she had known that it was Ashlyn. Still, nothing had prepared her for this bizarre scene. Ashlyn was using one hand to maintain her grip on the jagged frame of the driver's side door and the other to slowly squeeze the life out of Griff. Her feet were raised up in the air behind her. She looked as if she were being held up by wires.

Griff's eyes were bulging. His foot, which had been on the accelerator, was now pressed to the floor. Kimberly was barely in control of the Tempo as they hurtled through the darkened road.

"Yo, Kilpatrick!" Ashlyn howled. "What's the deal? I thought you and your boyfriend here were coming to our little *party!* You weren't going to stand us up, now were you? I mean, if that's the case, I guess we'll just have to bring the party to you!"

Suddenly, the headlights of an approaching car cut through the darkness. Kimberly aimed the Tempo directly for it.

"Oh no, you don't!" Ashlyn said, suddenly releasing her hold on Griff's throat as she attempted to wrestle with Kimberly for control of the wheel.

Griff gasped for air and grabbed the wheel with both hands. He jerked the wheel to the right, attempting to pass as close to the other car as possible. They were almost on top of the other vehicle now. It was a white family van. The driver honked frantically. Griff did not ease up on the accelerator.

With a curse, Ashlyn let go of the steering wheel and fell away. Griff saw her hit the ground and knew that the van would strike her at any second. Then a blur shot across the road and the van flew past. Ashlyn had been spirited away to safety by the gray horse. Griff slowed the car.

Still think I'm crazy? Kimberly wanted to ask, but the words would not come. Griff's face was bloody; she knew he was suffering.

They had no time to recover from the attack. Ahead, on the road, the gray horse appeared once again. This time, it wasn't standing still. It began to gallop directly at the car, Ashlyn on its back. Kimberly urged Griff to maintain a steady speed. She didn't want to play chicken with an illusion.

Instants before the fender came within striking distance of the horse, they realized their mistake. This wasn't another ghost image. It was for real. The gray horse leaped at the front windshield of the Tempo. One of the creature's hooves crashed through the glass and struck Griff as he tried to twist out of the way. It caught him on the side of the head with a sharp *crack*. Then its other hooves connected with the car and it somehow galloped over the roof and leaped off the trunk, back onto the road. They could hear Ashlyn's hysterical laugh the entire time.

Griff collapsed, his bloody head falling into Kimberly's lap.

He's dead, Kimberly thought. No, please God, no!

Griff's foot fell from the accelerator and the car sailed forward, caught by its momentum. Finally, it glided to a stop.

Griff was dead. He was dead and it was all her fault.

Suddenly, Kimberly heard his ragged breathing above her own sobs.

In the rear view mirror, Kimberly could see Ashlyn and the Sentinel approaching the car at a leisurely trot. Nikki and Tanya had reappeared beside them.

Kimberly looked through the shattered windshield, finally becoming aware of the shower of glass that had also rained upon her. She shook her head and glass fragments fell from her jacket and hair like deadly flakes of ice.

They were at a junction. Kimberly recognized the other road. Thirteen Bends. Not far from the Night Owl Club. She thought of the young waitress from the club, and a strange sense came over her that if anyone could help her, it was this woman.

In a sudden, desperate frenzy, Kimberly released the seat belt holding Griff in place. He was much bigger than she was and his limp body was dead weight. Still, Kimberly thought she could use what might be left of her unnatural strength to lift him up, slide beneath him, and take his place behind the wheel. Halfway through the task, her strength failed her and she found herself wedged under Griff's unconscious body. She couldn't breathe. He was pressing the air from her lungs. In a last, frantic effort, Kimberly shoved at her boyfriend, then gasped as he flopped forward, his head striking the dash. Kimberly moaned. She was aware of Ashlyn and the others laughing like banshees at her awkward attempts.

Squeezing herself to one side, Kimberly shoved Griff again; his body wavered then came down upon her. She could hear catcalls from the Predators.

They were much closer now than they had been a moment ago.

God, we've got to get out of this, we've got to, Kimberly chanted in her head.

Again, Kimberly pushed Griff away from her. His body sagged and his forehead struck the passenger head rest. She was in the driver's seat now, but Griff's legs were still wedged in the gap beneath the steering wheel, with his body twisted at an unnatural angle. Kimberly feared that she was going to kill him before she could save him.

Ashlyn's insane laughter came again to Kimberly. The Predators were almost beside the car. Desperately, Kimberly jammed her feet over Griff's and pressed the accelerator. Griff's body nearly flopped over her again, she used her right hand to hold it away as she steered with her left.

The laughter of the Predators suddenly ceased as the car rolled forward. Kimberly heard their rapid footfalls and knew they were suddenly racing for her. Kimberly floored the accelerator, turning sharply onto Thirteen Bends.

The glowing red eyes of the Sentinel followed for a time, then fell away. Maybe that last stunt had drained the creature or maybe it simply had no desire to travel on this road. For whatever reason, Kimberly knew that they had escaped — at least for now. Soon, she was pulling into the parking lot of the club.

Jenny was already waiting.

Twenty-eight

The club was closed. It was as if they had been expected. Jake took Griff in the back of the club and laid him down on a long leather couch. He proceeded to treat Griff's wounds with the professional detachment of a medic during wartime.

"Is he going to be all right?" Kimberly asked frantically as Jake finished cleaning and dressing the last of Griff's cuts.

"Of course he is," Jake groused. "Do you really think I want the bother of explaining to the police why some kid ended up dying in my club? And what do you think that would do for business? This place has a bad enough reputation."

Griff moaned and tried to sit up. Jake forced him back.

"Don't make a liar out of me, son. Stay put if you want to get better."

"It's all right, sweetheart," Kimberly said as she knelt beside Griff and took his hand. "Do what Mr. Demos says. We're going to be fine."

"The others—" he gasped.

"They won't come in here," Jenny said with a tone of finality. Her statement defied all logic, but so had much of what Kimberly had experienced in the past weeks. If Jenny said they were safe here, Kimberly believed her.

"You and I should talk," Jenny said to Kimberly.

Griff did not protest as Kimberly kissed him gently and told him that she would be close. Jake promised to stay with Griff, though he hardly seemed thrilled at the prospect. Then he called to his daughter.

"Don't forget the agreement," Jake said in a low voice.

Jenny nodded gravely and led Kimberly from the room. They went to the main section of the club and sat down at one of the booths.

"I'm sorry I was so awful to you," Kimberly said earnestly. "You didn't deserve the things I said in the parking lot the other night."

"Already forgotten. You weren't exactly yourself. Look, why don't you just tell me everything."

Kimberly nodded. She began to recount her experiences at the Cooper Riding Academy, the torments inflicted upon her by Sharon, her friendship with Ashlyn, and her relationship with Griff. She explained her dreams and nightmares, the growing shift in her attitude toward herself and those around her, and the horrors in which she had become involved.

"I know we can't go to the police," Kimberly said. "Ashlyn will find some way to turn it all around and make it look as if *Griff* were responsible for the missing kids, and for Sharon's and Gregory's deaths."

"I'm afraid there isn't much that I'll be able to do for you, either," Jenny said gently. "My father and I entered into an agreement when we came here. The degree to which we're allowed to be active in these matters is extremely limited."

"An agreement?" Kimberly asked. "With whom?"

Jenny looked away and smiled. Her expression made it clear there was no way she would answer that question.

"So what does that mean, exactly?" Kimberly asked, the sense of hope which had gripped her from the moment she and Griff had been led into the club quickly fading.

"I can advise you, but I can't go into battle for you."

Battle. That was a hell of a way to put it, Kimberly thought. Hundreds of years ago, it would have been normal to use that phrase in everyday conversation. Not now.

"It's not completely hopeless," Jenny said softly. "You did manage to get something away from the school, didn't you? You have it with you. It must be something pretty important for your friends to go after you like that."

"You think they want the book?" Kimberly asked, sud-

153

denly reminded of the dead weight in her pocket. She unzipped her jacket and reached inside to get the ancient diary. "But I can't read it. It's in some other language."

"Let me see." Jenny held out her hands and Kimberly passed the crumbling book to her with great care. Jenny opened it to a page at random and smiled. "I'm surprised you don't recognize the language of your own people."

"I'm sorry?" Kimberly asked.

Jenny began to flip through the pages. She stopped and scanned certain passages, then moved on almost feverishly. Absently, she said, "Your last name is Kilpatrick. Scottish. Just like your friend, Ashlyn."

"I wish you'd stop calling her that. She's not my friend. I told you what she did to me. And to others."

"I don't know. Friends do favors for one another, right?" Jenny asked as she continued to speed through the journal. Her fingers moved so quickly over the passages she chose to read that Kimberly found it hard to believe Jenny was actually absorbing any information.

"I guess."

"Well, if what I'm getting out of this book is to be believed, Ashlyn did you a big favor by leaving this out in the open, where you could get at it. If she really weren't your friend, she would have locked this thing away somewhere. Or burned it."

"Why? What's it say?" Kimberly said, some trace of her earlier enthusiasm returning.

"It's a diary written centuries ago by a woman named Victoria McConnel."

"Same last name as Ashlyn."

"Uh-huh. So how much do you know about Ashlyn's background?"

"Not much. Her parents were killed in an accident. They had money. Lots of it, the way Ashlyn talked."

"Apparently it's pretty old money," Jenny said.

"How old?"

"Ever see the movie *Highlander?*"

"Uh—yeah," Kimberly said, suddenly picturing Jenny sitting down in front of the television with some microwave popcorn and a rented video. The idea that this woman could be her savior suddenly moved far away.

"Remember the part where you were taken into the past and shown the ancient clans?"

Kimberly nodded.

"Well, let's just say that Victoria was married to that era's Donald Trump."

"Oh."

"The problem is, she found out how the McConnel family had made their fortune. It wasn't a wonderful thing to learn. Getting back to Ashlyn, does she have any living relatives?"

"None, according to her. She inherits everything when she's twenty-one."

"Then it all starts again," Jenny said absently.

"*What* all starts again?"

Jenny looked up at Kimberly. "I'm sorry. I'll try to be a little less circumspect."

"You could just tell me what's in the journal."

"I could. Have you ever heard the phrase, willing suspension of disbelief?"

"Uh, yeah. I guess. Why?"

"You're going to need it."

Twenty-nine

Jenny explained that the McConnel clan had not always been so fortunate. They had been struggling to survive, like so many others, until one of Ashlyn's ancestors made a deal with a terrible creature that promised wealth beyond his imagination if he worshipped it and supplied it with the blood of innocent children. Ashlyn's ancestor agreed. The family fortunate grew and both the McConnels and the nightmare creature they served thrived.

One day, Victoria McConnel, a violet-eyed beauty who had married into the family, discovered the family's blood heritage. She loved her husband, though, and could not believe that he was as violent and terrible as the McConnels who had come before him. To Victoria, her husband was a gentle man who had been enslaved by evil, and she saw it as her duty to free him.

Victoria's family had a history of magic, and so she devised a means to capture the creature. When her attempt to ensnare the creature failed, and her husband was about to suffer the monster's wrath as punishment for her actions, Victoria sacrificed her own life to save his. The very concept of self-sacrifice, of a love so pure and unselfish, was alien and abhorrent to the creature. It was overcome, vanquished by her final act, and its essence was captured in a sculpture she had created for this very eventuality.

"The final entry in the journal was written by Victoria's husband after her death," Jenny said. "Clearly, her belief in her husband's goodness was well-founded. In the entry, he swears he will keep the sculpture safe and that the monster will never again be released upon mankind. All of his descendants will be charged with the sacred duty of preserving the sculpture and serving as caretakers of the beast within." Jenny looked carefully at Kimberly.

"I think Ashlyn got a small part of her inheritance early."

"The statue."

"Right. Her parents may not have instructed her properly in her duties before they died, or she may not have believed their story. I think that once Ashlyn had the statue, the creature found some way to communicate with her."

"Her dreams," Kimberly said. "It can reach into a person's dreams. It did that with me."

"Okay. Maybe through her dreams. In any event, Ashlyn was seduced by the creature's promises and once again released it into the world."

"Look, could we stop calling this thing, 'the creature.' I mean, what exactly *is* it?"

"In every culture there is some kind of water spirit."

"Kind of like every country has its own version of werewolves and vampires, all that stuff," said Kimberly.

"Right," Jenny said.

"In Russia it's called the Rusalka. In Japan, the Ningyro. The recurring image of the gray horse makes me think of the Kelpie of Scottish mythology, and that fits, considering Ashlyn's bloodline. The legends concerning these water spirits may appear to be very different from one another, but when you strip away each society's particular trappings, they all have certain things in common. According to ancient lore, these creatures are generally tied to a particular body of water. In Victoria's diary, she talked about a lake near her castle, one that was rumored to have been inhabited by demons."

"So how did this—I dunno—Kelpie get out of the lake in Scotland and end up in Cooper Hollow?"

"These creatures have the power to disassociate themselves from the waters that are their home and live on to seek new victims elsewhere. That's what they say, anyway."

"What *they* say? Who's 'they?' " Kimberly asked, picturing Jenny somehow learning all of this in some dark, cobweb strewn classroom in some faraway land. Robed, wizened figures crowded around her, chants filled the ancient halls.

"The experts. I had to do a paper on mythology in college," said Jenny. "The New York Public Library has tons of information on this stuff."

"Oh." Kimberly suddenly felt very stupid. Then she asked, "You didn't answer my question. How could it have gotten here?"

"I told you before. Its spirit was captured in the statue. The statue was sent to Ashlyn. She released it."

"All right. This thing, this horse that drowns children, is a 'Kelpie.' What exactly is that?"

"The nightmare horse *may* be a Kelpie. Or it may be something else, something that inspired the Kelpie legends but only conforms to them in part."

"Fine, but what's a *Kelpie?*"

"A creature so repulsive, so impossible in its many aspects, that to look fully upon it would drive any mortal insane. Have you read anything by H.P. Lovecraft?"

"No."

"Seen the movies *Reanimator* or *From Beyond?*"

"I saw part of *From Beyond* on HBO. It was pretty gross. I turned it off."

"That was based on Lovecraft. He wrote about incredible monsters from other dimensions that came to our world and demanded to be worshipped. The Kelpie's like that."

"Okay," Kimberly said, finding her "willing suspension of disbelief" getting stretched to the limit.

"The monster can change its shape. The *Scottish Kelpie* was known to appear as a magnificent gray horse that lured its victims to their deaths. I think Ashlyn and her friends are the creature's handmaidens. They serve it, though it allows them to see themselves as its master."

"More like equal partners, the way Ashlyn puts it." Kimberly thought about this. "Maybe if I could convince them that they're being used, they might help us. Maybe—"

"I wouldn't count on it," Jenny said sharply.

158

Kimberly's tiny ledge of hope was crumbling beneath her. "You don't know these girls the way I do," she argued. "If they think they're being controlled, they won't put up with it. They'll fight back. I know they will."

"That may not be possible," Jenny said in a voice that was not to be challenged.

"What is it you're not telling me?" Kimberly asked.

"There is a way," Jenny said, ignoring her question. "Do you want to hear it?"

"Yes," Kimberly whispered.

"The spell Victoria used to capture the creature is written in this book. It worked once, it can work again."

"But—Victoria had to *die* for it to work." Kimberly was haunted by the story Jenny had told. Victoria had been forced to sacrifice herself to save the man she loved from the creature's punishment. Kimberly couldn't imagine allowing further harm to come to Griff, but she also couldn't predict how she would react if she were forced to make the decision Victoria McConnel had been forced to make.

"Find the shattered pieces of the statue that once contained the beast," Jenny said. "If you can find them, the spell may work without the need for a sacrifice."

"That means going back to school. They'll be waiting for me."

"No," Jenny said. "They're at the lake."

"Come on," Kimberly said. "Aren't we taking this 'willing suspension of disbelief' thing a little too far? You expect me to believe—"

Jenny's hand suddenly clamped on her wrist. Kimberly pulled back, frightened, but Jenny did not release her hold. The blond woman looked directly forward, but did not appear to see Kimberly. She was seeing something else.

"The photographs in your room at home," Jenny said in a dreamy voice, her eyes suddenly appearing glassy and unfocused. "The ones that burned. The ones of your real parents. Your uncle never wanted to see them. He said that he didn't want to be reminded of the loss."

"Wait a minute. Stop," Kimberly said, suddenly overcome by fear, tears springing from nowhere to well up in her eyes.

"But every time he looked at you he *was* reminded—of his own guilt. He *knew* the pipes beneath your parents' restaurant were bad. They had asked him for the money to fix them and he refused to give it. He told them he had poured enough of his money into their losing proposition. He told them that they should cut their losses and get jobs in the real world. That's what he told them."

"They knew?" Kimberly asked, horrified. A single tear rolled down her cheek. "They *knew* something could happen?"

"Your mother and father believed it to be a remote possibility. They thought they could afford to wait until business got better. The outlay would have ruined them." Jenny's gaze fastened on Kimberly. "You know all this. You just won't admit it to yourself."

Suddenly, a long buried memory rose up to the forefront of Kimberly's thoughts. She remembered overhearing a conversation between her parents and her uncle . . . Yes. Everything Jenny had said was true.

"There's more that you should see," Jenny said, "more that you should understand—"

"No!" Kimberly cried, wrenching her arm from Jenny's grasp. What Jenny had shown her couldn't possibly be true. Her parents *couldn't* have put themselves and their daughter at risk like that. But deep inside, Kimberly knew that it *was* the truth, and that there were other truths she had denied. The memories clawed at the surface of her consciousness, but Kimberly forced them away.

None of it mattered. Kimberly had failed to warn her parents of the smell in the basement. If she had, they would have known instantly what that smell had been and would have left the restaurant in time. The revelation of their knowledge of the faulty pipes didn't make things any better.

"I wasn't trying to hurt you," Jenny said softly. "But you have a weakness Ashlyn and the others can use. So long as you keep lying to yourself about what happened with your parents—"

"Stop it," Kimberly said, crying openly. She snatched a cloth napkin from the table and wiped at her tears.

Jenny shuddered, her eyes suddenly returning to their former sharpness. With an unexpected tenderness, she reached across the table and took Kimberly's hand. "There are some things that are better to just take on faith. Ashlyn, Nikki, and Tanya are at the lake. If you move quickly, you should be able to get to school and get out again before they head back. I can't explain how I know, how I can sense that they're at the lake, but it's the truth. Do you believe me?"

Kimberly nodded. The tears were still moist on her face. "Yes. I believe you."

Thirty

Jake grudgingly allowed Kimberly to take his truck. Kimberly had a hard time picturing Jake Demos doing anything in a manner that was less than grudging.

"I'm not going to be able to get into their rooms," Kimberly had told Jenny. "Not without breaking the doors down somehow. And even if I could do that, I'd wake up everyone on the floor."

"You have a key," Jenny said, tapping the side of her head. "*This* key opens all locks."

"What do you mean?"

"They've given you some of their power. Use it."

Kimberly was not entirely certain she still had the power, but she trusted Jenny, and was willing to give it a try. Griff objected to Kimberly going alone, but he was clearly in no shape to accompany her. He railed at Jenny for refusing to go with Kimberly, but Jenny told him that it was not possible.

Kimberly parked several blocks away from the school grounds and snuck in through the usual secret route. She was halfway across the lawn when she heard the *chuffing* of a horse behind her. Fighting her every instinct to freeze, Kimberly turned slowly. It was not the gray horse. She recognized this one. It was the brown horse she usually rode, the one that had taken Lightning's place.

The animal was terrified. Shapes rose out of the darkness. Other horses wandered into her line of view.

What had happened here tonight, she wondered. Had the horses been set free or had they broken free? Kimberly pictured the horses breaking down the wooden barriers of their stalls and attacking the barn doors en masse.

162

No. Even if it had been possible for them to escape in that way, they would have made enough noise to draw out half the staff and wake the entire school. Their movements even now were eerily silent. They seemed to be waiting for something.

It wasn't until the first of the horses charged her that she realized they had been waiting for *her*.

Kimberly dove out of the way, narrowly avoiding the brown horse. Its eyes revealed no malice, only fear. The animal had been placed under some kind of spell. Another horse, pure white, darted in her direction, feinted to the right, and then attacked with a savage burst of speed. Kimberly darted out of the way and collided with the flank of a tan horse.

The horse whirled around and butted her ribs with its huge head. Kimberly was knocked off her feet. She tried to rise and saw the hooves of another animal approaching. Spinning over and over she avoided the hooves, and saw that the other animals were closing around her. She scrambled to her feet and faced her attackers.

In all her life, the greatest peace and freedom she had ever found had been on the backs of horses. Now Ashlyn had taken even that sanctuary from her. She had corrupted Kimberly's last refuge.

Kimberly had a concern even beyond surviving this strange gauntlet. Eventually, the sounds of the horses would wake someone at the school. The person would look out and see her. That couldn't happen. Maybe she could use her power to make herself invisible like the Predators had shown her before. Kimberly concentrated, keeping the thought that she was now invisible in her mind, and attempted to navigate through the mass of horses.

The animals were not attacking. Was it possible the magic *was* working and that the horses couldn't see her either?

No. Another horse broke from the pack and galloped straight for her. It was nightmare black, horribly reminiscent of the mount that had taken Sharon to her death.

Kimberly waited until the last possible second and darted out of the way. The creature seemed to know instinctively in which direction she would move and corrected its own course to match hers. Then, it struck her down. She lay on the ground, gasping for breath, afraid that the black horse would rise up above her at any second. She glimpsed the side of its head as it passed by. Bones jutted from its ruined flesh. Bubbling white foam leaked from the corner of its mouth. The creature's tongue lagged to one side and its eyes were rolled up into the back of its head.

It *was* Sharon's horse.

Breath returned to Kimberly in a shattering gasp. She brought herself unsteadily to her feet and passed through another half dozen horses that milled about, their heads swinging zombie-like from one side to another as, presumably, they searched for her. The black horse had lost interest in her. Kimberly continued to walk, looking over her shoulder for the black horse to appear once more, when she bumped into something. She whirled around and nearly screamed.

"Invisibility. Nice trick," a thick, guttural voice whispered. "But they have other senses. Like *smell*."

It was Sharon. A white frock hung unevenly from her twisted shoulders, revealing enough of her chest for Kimberly to make out the V of the autopsy scar. Her head hung at a strange angle and only part of her face remained on the bone.

Kimberly fought down the urge to vomit. This thing wasn't really Sharon. It was her body, all right, at least what was left of it, but that meant very little. The grinning monstrosity before her was just a weapon that Ashlyn was using against her. At least now she understood how the animals had been released.

Sharon sniffed the air in an exaggerated motion. "I think they're on to you."

I doubt it, Kimberly thought. Sharon's smell and the noxious odor drifting off her head mount was a fairly lethal combination. The horses' senses would be confused.

"And if that fails, just remember that *I* can see you."

Sharon took a step forward, causing Kimberly to retreat a step. Kimberly glanced back at the crowd of horses. She was near the edge of the gathering. One last, frantic run and she might beat them back to school.

"You don't really believe that, do you?" Sharon asked, sensing Kimberly's thoughts. "Or that I'll be slow, like zombies in the movies?"

Sharon darted one way then the other in lightning quick motions, her hands all the while at her sides. Kimberly didn't want Sharon to raise them. She knew what had happened to them. Again, realizing her thoughts, Sharon brought the sharp, bony stumps that had once been her hands into view. Like carving knives. They looked like carving knives.

"I think we should have a long discussion, but there probably won't be time for that," Sharon said, moving toward Kimberly at a steady pace. "But there's one thing I want you to know. It wasn't me. I didn't try to burn down your house. I didn't destroy your precious pictures. I wouldn't even know about that except that after I died I was called back, and you find things out when you cross over.

"The thing is, it was your friend Ashlyn all along. Her and her friends. You hounded me right into my grave for *nothing*. Now I'm going to settle the score."

Kimberly knew that she should have been surprised, but she wasn't. Ashlyn had manipulated her from the beginning.

"I'm sorry," Kimberly said.

"Not as sorry as you're going to be," Sharon replied, still advancing. "You're mine, Kilpatrick. Mine!"

A part of Kimberly wanted the nightmare to be over so badly that she almost held still as Sharon stabbed in her direction with the rapier-like bones of her arms. Part of her felt that she *deserved* to be punished for Sharon's torment and her death. But there was something in Sharon's one good eye, something in her tone that seemed to be pleading for release. Sharon wanted vengeance, but not on Kimberly. They shared a mutual enemy, one that

Sharon was powerless to fight.

I didn't kill Sharon, Kimberly had told Ashlyn. No, Ashlyn had replied, the gray horse killed her, but it was responding to Kimberly's desires. That's it, Kimberly realized. I can control these horses, too!

Sharon charged at Kimberly, driving her into the midst of the animals. She won't give me time to think, Kimberly realized. I can't *use* the power if I can't concentrate!

Kimberly stopped running. She held her ground and Sharon drove her talon-like arms at her. Then she grabbed each stump and held them over Sharon's head. As she had wagered, Sharon's strength was no match for Kimberly's.

"No!" Sharon screamed, but Kimberly was beyond hearing her. She was beyond the fear and revulsion she felt at actually touching this walking corpse. All her attention was trained on a single task.

The horses gathered around them. One of them took a running start and slammed into Sharon from behind. She grunted and a terrible cracking sound came from her arms. Kimberly kept her composure as Sharon's upper arms snapped off in her hands and the corpse fell twitching to the ground.

A cry sounded from the other side of the gathering of horses. A pitiful animal whinnying that might have been a plea for release. The black horse. Many of the living horses had gathered around it. The others came for Sharon.

Kimberly ran from the circle of animals, ignoring Sharon's cries as the hooves of the beasts crashed down on her, shattering her body! Kimberly couldn't tell if they were cries of fear or of gratitude. Nothing would be left of Sharon's corpse by the time the others arrived. The animals had made their choice between the living and the dead.

Entering the school, Kimberly stayed perfectly still as a half dozen people rushed past her to see what was happening with the horses outside. Then she stole up the stairs and went to Ashlyn's room. It was locked, but, by concentrating, she was able to move the tumblers. The lock disengaged. She opened the door and went inside.

She had taken no more than three steps before the door slammed shut and someone grabbed her.

Thirty-one

"I really thought you were smarter than this," Ashlyn said.

This was impossible, Kimberly thought. Jenny had assured her that Ashlyn and the others would be at the lake, not the school. The waitress had been right about so many other things, how could she be wrong about *this?*

As if sensing her thoughts, Ashlyn said, "Your friend has power. I won't deny that. But she's way out of her league with us. We anticipated that she would use her *sight* to keep watch over us and so we made her see exactly what we wanted her to see."

Kimberly was backed against the wall. Nikki and Tanya stood waiting for her to make a move. This time they were ready for her. Kimberly was certain she could not get away from them unless they willed it.

Leaning back against the bedpost, Ashlyn said, "You came here looking for what remains of the statue. Sorry to disappoint you, but there's nothing left of it. Our lord had been a prisoner for centuries. His essence had fused with the statue. When he was released from his confinement, the magical bonds holding him in the form of the statue were loosed and he transformed to his true state. It wasn't like a genie escaping from a bottle, leaving broken pieces everywhere. Our lord and his prison had become one and the same."

Kimberly felt as if she were once again on that crumbling ledge. This time it gave way beneath her and she found herself tumbling down into an abyss of hopelessness. Suddenly, her fall was arrested in mid-flight.

She was still alive. They could have just killed her. There must be something they wanted.

The book. Victoria's journal.

"You're beginning to catch on," Ashlyn said. "I know you weren't stupid enough to keep it with you. Where is it?"

Kimberly felt her courage returning slowly. "You don't need me to tell you that."

"I know you took it into the club. Where is it now? Where did Demos and his daughter take it?"

Ashlyn obviously had some kind of link with the journal. Apparently, she was able to track its location with the magic she had been given by her master. If it had left the club, she would know it, wouldn't she? Or did Jake and Jenny have ways of deceiving the creature Ashlyn served?

"You don't understand about that place, do you?" Ashlyn said. "Maybe that's just as well. Anyway, it doesn't really matter where they may have taken it. Wherever it is, they can get it back."

"If it's so important, why'd you just leave it laying around?" Kimberly asked.

Ashlyn became livid. Her eyes seemed to blaze. "Don't you dare criticize me!" she wailed.

Kimberly liked the sudden feeling of power she had acquired. "Why didn't you burn it if it was so dangerous? That was pretty stupid."

Moving so quickly she could only be registered as a blur, Ashlyn leapt forward and drove Kimberly's head against the wall. Kimberly cried out in agony and surprise. Pain lanced through her head and she saw a kaleidoscope of colors explode before her eyes. Ashlyn pressed her fingers into the hollows of Kimberly's cheeks and began to squeeze.

"I tried to burn it," Ashlyn snarled. "But it always came back. I tried to hide it. Guess what? *It came back.* I tore the pages out of the binding and put them through a shredder. That didn't help. No matter what I did with that damned thing, it came back. That's why when it was gone I didn't think anything of it. But our lord isn't pleased. Therefore, neither am I."

Ashlyn released her hold on Kimberly.

169

"You want the book," Kimberly said, rubbing her sore jaw. Three words she had heard in class a million times rang in her mind: *Knowledge is power.* She finally understood the true meaning of that saying.

"No kidding." Ashlyn sat on the bed. "My lord has instructed me to bargain with you. You have something we want, we have something you want. Let's deal."

"All right," Kimberly said, though she had no real intention of dealing with Ashlyn and her friends. She wondered what would happen if she began to scream at the top of her lungs. Trying to explain all this to Mrs. Alcott was a ridiculous idea. The police would be of no help, either. Jake and Jenny were bound not to interfere, for some bizarre reason. She had to find some way to prevent Ashlyn and the others from going after Griff at the club.

"Give us the book and we promise to leave both you and your precious boyfriend alone," Ashlyn said.

"That's it? That's your best offer?"

"You've rejected everything else we could give you. Our lord would have been very generous to you. You turned your back on everything we tried to give you. We offered you love and acceptance, money and power, freedom and happiness. You betrayed us. We have no wish to be insulted again."

"Your offer's not worth anything. The second you have the book, you'll do to us what you did to Gregory Rose."

"That was different."

"I don't see how," Kimberly said. "He stepped over the line, right? He rejected you, just like I did."

"I wasn't the only one who wanted Rose dead. You were happy when you found out he had died. Admit it."

"Yes," Kimberly said. There was no sense in denying it. She could still feel pain in her jaw where he had struck her.

"I did it for you," Ashlyn said. "I saved you. I made you into what you always dreamed of becoming."

"You never did anything for *me*. You did it all for yourself."

"We made your heart's desire come true," Ashlyn said coldly. "You wanted your parents back, we gave them to

170

you. You can have them with you all the time, you can go back and change the way things worked out—"

"It's all just lies!" Kimberly screamed. "I want the truth. I want reality, not illusions."

Ashlyn laughed bitterly. "You already know the truth. You're just too scared to see it. Illusions are all you can handle."

Kimberly tried to ignore Ashlyn's words, though the memory she had managed to suppress in the club earlier that evening once again attempted to surface.

Ashlyn looked away sourly. "We're the same, you and me. You're just too stupid to admit that, even to yourself. That's going to cost you."

"I'm waiting for another offer."

"There is none," Ashlyn said as she rushed forward and grabbed Kimberly's wrist. "We're going back to the club."

Kimberly's momentary sense of bravado faded at once. "Griff isn't going to give you the book."

"Of course he is," Ashlyn said as she snatched a straight razor from her dresser top and put it against Kimberly's throat. "Given the right motivation, I'm sure he won't be any problem at all."

Kimberly could think of only one final argument to use with her former friends. Jenny had warned her that this would be a useless tack, but she had nothing to lose.

"Why are you doing what this thing wants?" she asked, her gaze flickering from Ashlyn to Nikki to Tanya. "This thing's using all three of you. You're not partners with it. You're slaves."

"I don't need to listen to this," Nikki said. "Let's get out of here."

"No," Ashlyn said. "She said she wanted the truth. Let's show her the truth."

With a crooked smile, Tanya grabbed Kimberly by the hair and forced the girl's head against her chest.

"Listen. Listen *close*," Tanya said.

For a moment, all Kimberly could hear was the thunderous beating of her own heart. Then, she realized the sound of her own heart was the *only* beating she heard.

171

Tanya's flesh was ice cold. Her chest was not rising and falling with breaths.

Tanya was not alive. Kimberly tried to pull away, but her former friend held her tight.

It killed her, Kimberly thought, it killed them all and brought them back to serve it. This is what Jenny had been reluctant to tell her. The waitress had correctly assumed that Kimberly would not have believed Ashlyn and the others to be little more than reanimated corpses.

Too much. It was too much for her mind to bear.

"Poor little Kimberly," Nikki said in a taunting voice. "Just couldn't handle the pressure, could you? All three of us gave up boys that loved us. My boyfriend was raised on a farm. He loved horses. He got on the back of the Sentinel and thought he was going for the ride of his life. He didn't know how right he was."

"We've all given up so much," Tanya said. "But look how much we've gained. It would have been better for you to have joined us. So sad."

"You're a *reject*," Ashlyn said. "You don't have any guts. If you did, your parents would still be alive right now."

The words nearly crippled Kimberly. The fight went out of her.

Ashlyn pulled Kimberly away from Tanya and steered her to the door. "Nothing you say could ever cause us to betray our lord. He has given us the kiss of eternity. We'll remain like this forever. Young and beautiful. Powerful."

Slaves, Kimberly thought, but there was no point in saying it.

"Let's go," Ashlyn snarled. "We have a lot to do tonight . . ."

172

Thirty-two

Ashlyn refused to go near Jake's truck. Instead, they took the car Tanya had allowed Kimberly to use. The car did not misbehave with a dead girl behind the wheel. Now that the charade was over, the girls had dropped the pretense of being a closely-knit group of friends. They were dead, they were servants, that's all there was to it.

On the drive, Kimberly could not keep herself from thinking about Victoria's sacrifice. The woman loved her husband more than her own life. Kimberly knew that she loved Griff and would do anything to save him, but she was terrified of becoming another handmaid to the creature.

Kimberly also thought of Ashlyn's cryptic statement just before they left the dorm: *You already know the truth. You're just too scared to see it.*

Deep down, a part of Kimberly understood what Ashlyn meant, but Kimberly would not listen to its urgent plea.

They reached the Night Owl Club and parked before the unmarked entrance. Ashlyn honked the horn until the door opened and Jenny stepped out.

"You can come in if you want," Jenny said brightly. "I'll make some hot cocoa and we can talk this whole thing out."

The facetiousness in the waitress' voice did not escape Ashlyn. "Yeah, and maybe we can put on 'The Chipmunks Christmas Album' and talk about which of the Simpsons we like best."

Jenny shrugged as Kimberly was hauled out of the car. "Just a thought."

Griff suddenly appeared in the doorway. A bandage

had been wrapped around his head. The book was clutched in his hand.

Jake Demos popped up beside him. "Just tell me you didn't trash my truck."

Jenny's expression went cold. "We have more important issues to deal with."

"More important to *you,* maybe."

"Your truck's fine," Ashlyn said. "You think we'd actually touch something that belonged to one of *your* kind?"

Jake laughed. "No, I suppose not." The older man shook his head and receded into the club's interior.

"I'm sure you've dealt with this kind of scene before," Ashlyn said to Jenny. "But for Griff's sake, I'll lay it all out."

Griff shifted uncomfortably and gripped the door jamb. He fixed his gaze on Kimberly, who stood less than a dozen feet away, with Tanya and Nikki on either side of her. Nikki had taken out the straight razor and placed it at Kimberly's throat.

"Here's how it works," Ashlyn said. "Give us the book and we'll spare your girlfriend's life."

"Griff—" Kimberly began, but her words were cut off by the sting of the razor, which bit into the flesh of her throat.

"Oh, and her job is to urge you to be noble and refuse. After all, once we have the book, what reason do we have for keeping our word? We'll kill both of you, anyway."

"That about sum it up?" Nikki asked, pressing lightly on the blade.

Kimberly closed her eyes in response. The spell, she thought. Open the book and read the spell. It's our only chance.

"Well," Ashlyn said, "take it from somebody who knows, there's nothing noble about being dead. Now let's get this over with."

"All right," Griff said, moving forward sluggishly.

Don't, Kimberly thought. For God's sake, Griff, don't!

He stopped before Ashlyn and put the book in her hands. "Happy?"

Ashlyn slid the journal into her jacket pocket. "Ecstatic."

She turned to Nikki. "Let her go."

Nikki hesitated, confused.

"You heard me, do it." The blade with withdrawn and Kimberly raced into Griff's arms. They held each other, and he whispered that it was over.

"Not really," Ashlyn said.

Griff and Kimberly looked to her sharply.

"Nothing's going to happen tonight," Ashlyn said. "Nothing except Tommy Bryant recanting his confession for the murder of Gregory Rose. He's going to admit that you paid him to confess so that the cops would be thrown off long enough for you to get out of town."

"You can't do that," Kimberly said.

"I can do anything. And why should Tommy go down for the crime? He didn't do it."

"Neither did Griff."

"That's not my problem," Ashlyn said. "It's yours."

"It was you. You killed Gregory Rose."

"With a little help from my friends," Ashlyn amended. "That's just the beginning of your troubles. There's also the question of Sharon's death."

"You're responsible for that, too."

"No kidding. But the police are going to find that Sharon's gear was tampered with. The reins sawed through. Who had motive? Why, Kimberly Kilpatrick, officer. What about opportunity? I saw her over by Sharon's stuff. Didn't think anything of it. Everyone knew that Sharon was lazy and didn't check her equipment every time she went out, like she was supposed to."

"I was with Ms. Saberhagen the whole time!" Kimberly cried.

"You really think getting her to tell a different story is going to be difficult?" Ashlyn asked. "I mean, everyone has their price."

"We know about you. We know what you're doing with the children," Kimberly threatened.

"As if anyone's going to believe you," Ashlyn said. Then she looked to Jenny. "Well, there's a few oddballs who might believe you, but they won't do anything about it.

175

They can't. They're too weak."

"Want to come in here and say that?" Jenny asked, motioning to the inside of the club with a grand sweeping gesture.

Ashlyn ignored her. "No, I think it's going to be more fun to have both of you locked up for the rest of your lives. And if we decide that what either of you says is too dangerous, well, accidents happen in prisons, right? Only the accident won't happen to the one who talks. It'll happen to the other one. That should keep you both quiet. Who knows, maybe in ten or twenty years, when you little idiots get out, I'll be able to put both of you to work for me."

From the far distance, a police siren lazily drifted in their direction.

"Oh, did I say Tommy's little reversal *would* happen?" Ashlyn asked. "Actually, it already has. The police are on their way here to get you. They're actually a little farther away than I'm letting on. Plenty of time for you two to run, if that interests you."

"No," Griff said. "This is what interests me."

A startling stream of arcane words burst from Griff's lips. Kimberly could not follow any of it; the language was alien to her. Nevertheless, she knew that it was the spell. Somehow Griff had learned it while she was back at the school.

The slight smile playing across Jenny's lips told Kimberly that she was mistaken. It was Jenny. She had placed the spell in Griff's mind.

Without warning, Tanya scooped up a large rock from the ground and ran at Griff. Kimberly moved to stop her, but icy hands gripped her from behind. Nikki. As the spell built to a crescendo, Tanya clubbed Griff on the wounded side of his head. The boy crumbled to his knees. Tanya raised the stone again, then stopped as the sound of nightmarish hooves cut through the night. Instants later, the gray horse appeared. Lifting Griff's weighty form without difficulty, Tanya draped Griff's unconscious body over the Sentinel's back. With a terrible scream, the horse raced into the night.

Kimberly had been screaming for Jenny to help, but the woman was no longer in the doorway. Nikki's grip was unbreakable. Twisting in Nikki's grasp, Kimberly was able to see a figure slam into Nikki from behind. Her captor's eyes rolled up into the back of her head and she released Kimberly as she tumbled to the ground. Tanya started forward and the figure that had attacked Nikki went after Tanya, grabbing her, holding her back.

It was *Ashlyn*.

"The keys are still in the ignition," Ashlyn screamed.

For a moment, Kimberly was frozen with confusion.

"Go! Do it, go!"

Breaking from her paralysis, Kimberly ran to the driver's side door, slipped behind the wheel, and tore out of the parking lot.

Thirty-three

No roads led directly to the lake. Kimberly lost sight of the gray horse seconds after she got on Thirteen Bends, but that didn't matter. She knew where it was taking Griff. In her dreams, she had been there dozens of times. She also knew that the Sentinel would wait for her.

She reached the intersection, crossed back to the road leading to Cooper Riding Academy and the next township over, and stopped when she came to where she had met Griff the first time. Abandoning the car on the shoulder of the road, Kimberly darted into the woods. In moments, she emerged from the woods and came to the sparkling waters of the lake. It felt strange to stand in this place for real after having done so dozens of times in her dreams. The gray horse was waiting, Griff's unconscious form draped across its back.

She started in the Sentinel's direction, but it moved back a few yards, its hooves sloshing through the water as it retreated into the lake.

"He's not really the one you want," Kimberly said softly. "I am, right?"

The beast swiveled its terrible head in her direction. Its blood-red eyes held her. The cold intelligence within them told her all she needed to know.

On the drive, Kimberly had come to understand why Ashlyn had allowed her to escape. This was not about Kimberly's battle with the other girls. It never had been. They were servants. Her fight was with the creature they served.

Now it had come to this, an age-old battle. Victoria McConnel, Ashlyn's ancestor, had been forced to choose between her own life and that of her beloved. Her sacrifice had saved that man, and it had helped to enslave the un-seen monster hiding within the lake. Tonight, it was Kim-berly's turn to choose between her own life and that of her beloved.

She considered stalling. Griff might come around. If he could complete the spell, they might both escape.

As if sensing her thoughts, the Sentinel backed further into the waters. The moment any such attempt began, the horse would throw Griff deep into the waters, where he would be dragged down without hesitation.

Victoria McConnel had been a grown woman when she had to choose between life and death. Kimberly was just a kid. It wasn't fair. How could she make such a decision?

"All right," Kimberly said tremblingly. "Let's do this be-fore I lose my nerve. I'll join you. You do to me what you did to the others. But you let him go, and everything Ashlyn said about ruining his life doesn't happen. Agreed?"

The Sentinel's burning red eyes pierced her. Its gaze was unwavering. Suddenly, it lowered its head in acquies-cence.

"What do I do?" Kimberly asked.

The gray horse swiveled its head in the direction of the lake. Kimberly understood. Just walk into the waters, she thought. Walk into the waters, stupid, and let it take you.

It sounded so easy. But for a moment she couldn't bring herself to take the first step. Then she did it, and then she was up to her knees in the waters. The placid surface of the lake began to turn violent, and she felt the waters churning around her legs. A slight depression opened up a few yards ahead and Kimberly guessed it was the eye of a maelstrom beginning to form.

You're coming to me, she thought. I'm doing this. I'm actually doing this. Only a few days ago she had con-vinced herself that she hated Griff enough to want him dead. Now she was willing to die in his place. What was it she had read in literature class? Something about love and hate being two sides of the same coin?

A few more steps. The waters came up to her hips. She thought of Griff. In her mind, she chanted, *I love you, sweetheart. I love you, baby. I love you.*

"Stop!" It was a voice calling from shore. A woman's voice. At first, Kimberly thought it was Jenny. Her friend must have decided to override whatever "agreement" she had made and had come to help her after all. But it wasn't Jenny's voice. It was a voice Kimberly had never heard before.

Turning, Kimberly saw Ashlyn standing on the store, Victoria McConnel's journal in her hands. The book was open and Ashlyn began reading from it. The voice that came from her lips was not her own. As she spoke, her eyes began to burn deep violet.

The Sentinel raced toward the shore, charging at Ashlyn. The violence of its sudden movements caused it to dislodge Griff from its back. He plunged into the waters, only a few feet deep—deep enough for someone to drown in. Kimberly made a move in his direction, but something grabbed her leg. Whatever had taken hold of her had a pulsing, slimy membrane, and felt like an old sock filled with rocks, twigs, and razor blades.

She refused to look down at it. Instead, she looked to where Griff had vanished under the waters. Suddenly, his head bobbed free of the surface then sank beneath once again. His right arm emerged from the waters now, flailing, then it, too, was gone. She could see that he was being dragged beneath the surface, a trail of air bubbles marking his journey toward the maelstrom.

On the shore, Ashlyn raised a hand and the animal stopped within only a few feet of her. It reared up and screamed in frustration, but Ashlyn continued to read.

Kimberly felt the *thing* that gripped her leg tug at her. She lost her balance and fell into the murky waters. The water was freezing. It was much colder than it had been a few seconds ago, or so it seemed. Underwater, Kimberly gasped as she saw a jagged rock reaching up for her face. Twisting out of the way, she felt ice water snaking into her lungs and tried desperately to free herself. But the more she struggled, the tighter the thing's hold on her.

Kimberly's fingers fastened on an old twisting root and she felt a sliver of hope. Then the root snapped off in her hands the way Sharon's bony arms had broken apart earlier that night. It was getting harder and harder to resist the urge to breathe. If she gave in to her body's desperate need, her lungs would fill with water and she would drown even faster.

The creature yanked her down. She was being raked against the rocks and the trash in the bottom of the lake as the thing pulled her in deeper.

Suddenly, the icy waters of the lake vanished. She found herself sitting on a hard wood floor. Kimberly gasped for breath, grateful to be alive. And then she realized where she had been taken.

No, not this, please!

She was in the restaurant her parents had owned. She saw her reflection in a mirror on the wall. She was a child again.

This isn't real, this isn't happening, I can't give in to this! It's showing me what I want to see! It's a lie!

"Kimberly?"

She whirled around and saw her mother. The woman knelt before Kimberly, taking her little girl's face in her warm hands. "What's wrong, honey?"

Suddenly, Kimberly could smell the fumes. Breathlessly, she said, "Downstairs! A terrible smell, like — *gas.*"

The older woman's face went white. "Tom! Tom, we've got to get out of here, now!"

Kimberly turned and saw her father enter the main serving room. "What is it?"

"Gas, downstairs, we've got to get out!"

There was no hesitation. Kimberly's mother took her hand and practically dragged her out of the restaurant. Her father was directly behind them. Tom Kilpatrick said, "Let's get to the pay phone on the corner."

They hurried to it and behind them came a terrible explosion. The force of the blast knocked them to the ground as glass exploded from nearby windows. Kimberly had

181

not been this close to the explosion all those years before. It had been only a muffled bang . . .

This isn't real!

But it felt real and, God help her, she wanted it to be real. More than anything in the world she wanted this. They were safe. All three of them were safe; they could be a happy family again.

Something was wrong. Kimberly felt the weight of someone's gaze upon her. She looked away from her parents, who were picking themselves up and brushing off the flakes of glass. On the opposite corner stood a boy with his hands in his pocket. He wore blue jeans and a leather jacket and he was handsome—

Griff.

Kimberly understood what was going on. She was drowning, dying, and the creature had almost won. This is how it lured its victims in their final moments, how it coaxed them into giving their souls to it.

I can't believe in this, not in any of this!

Griff pointed at something over her shoulder. Kimberly turned and, in the glass of the hardware store window next to her, saw an image form.

Why didn't that glass break? Keep thinking like that; this isn't real!

Suddenly, she felt strong hands on her shoulders. Griff. No, not really Griff. Some part of her mind cloaking itself in his form so that she would listen to it. Kimberly put her hands over his.

"In a way, you feel that you deserve this," Griff said. "You believe that you should be punished. As long as you think that way, you don't have a chance of winning. All this is a lie. What you believed happened all those years ago is a lie. Do you want to see the *truth?*"

"Yes," she whispered, both terrified and excited.

Unable to look away, Kimberly saw the surface of the unbroken glass cloud and transform.

Thirty-four

Kimberly saw the restaurant her parents owned. Once again, she saw her mother and father the way they had been minutes before their deaths.

A young girl, Kimberly almost ten years ago, was trying desperately to get their attention. She was going on and on about the funny smell downstairs, in the basement, but neither of her parents would listen.

"Maybe this'll shut you up," her dad said in exasperation. He went to a nearby storage room, unlocked it, and hauled out a shiny blue bicycle. "I didn't know where else to keep this so that you wouldn't see it sooner."

Kimberly went to the bicycle and touched it tentatively.

"All right? Happy Birthday, one day early. Now go and play. We've got work to do."

The sharpness of his tone caused the young Kimberly to bite her lower lip. Somehow keeping herself from crying, she walked the bicycle out of the restaurant, her father holding the door for her, and tried one last time to tell her father about the strange smell before he slammed the door in her face and locked it.

Kimberly looked away from the glass. Griff was gone. Her parents stood, silent and waiting. "No, that's not right, that's not how it happened at all."

But that was *exactly* how it had happened. That was why she was obsessed with having power, why she was the perfect recruit for the Predators.

My parents wouldn't listen to me, Kimberly thought. I tried to warn them and they wouldn't listen. I *didn't* want to see them one more time to say that I was sorry.

183

I've been *angry* with them. I've been angry with them for almost ten years because they *didn't listen to me.* Because I was just a kid and I didn't have the power to *make* them listen to me.

The images faded. Kimberly looked at herself in the glass and tried to wipe away her tears. She knew that for the first time she was not being manipulated. For the first time in so many years, Kimberly knew that she was confronting the truth.

Anger erupted within her. Her parents had *known* there was a problem. And then when she had tried to warn them that a crisis was near, they hadn't listened. They had been too busy worrying about their immediate concerns to listen to her warning. She had done her best and that was all anyone could ask.

Kimberly spun on her parents. "You should have listened to me! I could have saved you but you didn't *listen!*"

Her parents vanished. All of it vanished. It was an illusion that was no longer necessary.

Kimberly was drowning in the lake. She felt the air being pressed from her lungs and she *fought back.* Gathering all the anger she had been repressing for close to a decade, Kimberly turned her focused fury upon the creature.

In a last, frantic effort, Kimberly yanked herself into a fetal position, bringing her face and hands close to whatever it was that had captured her. She saw red, puckered flesh hanging off impossibly twisted bone, ropy muscles, and gooey slabs of pink and white mucus that looked unspeakably vile. Kimberly brought up the foot and a half long, curling section of root she had held onto and rammed it into the appendage that had taken hold of her. It screamed and she felt a startling wave of satisfaction as the monster loosed its hold on her.

Kimberly swam, her lungs about to collapse. She was dully aware of a shape coming near her, a thing that looked like a cross between a cockroach, an octopus, and an eighteen wheeler—only much worse. It had hundreds of mouths, a multitude of eyes, and wriggling appendages.

Arms pumping wildly, Kimberly broke the surface of the lake and gasped for air. Any second now, she expected the thing beneath the waters to grab at her again. She swam toward the shore, unmindful of anything but her own fear.

Slowly, reason came back to her. Griff had also been taken by the creature. On the shoreline, Ashlyn stood with her glowing violet eyes, reading from Victoria's journal in her strange, unearthly voice. The Sentinel stood before her, shuddering, anxious to get at her, but prevented by some force Kimberly could not understand. How much time had passed since she had been sucked under the water? Seconds? Minutes?

Again, she was faced with a choice. She could get away clean. She had seen this thing for what it was. Or, at least, she had seen enough of it to realize that there was nothing she could do to fight it. She had been incredibly lucky to get away from the monster.

But what would happen to Griff? Ashlyn was still reading Victoria's spell. She was reaching that same crescendo that Griff had been approaching when he had been attacked. Kimberly didn't know if the spell would work or not. And if it did, it would certainly come too late to save Griff from the monstrosity beneath the lake.

I can't go back, can't see it again, can't bear the feel of its touch, she thought frantically. Nevertheless, she turned, took a deep breath, and dove into the inky waters.

She could see nothing. The creature was down here. She knew that. At any moment the ebon veil of the waters would part and she would find herself within inches of the abomination. Kimberly swam on. She had to find Griff. She had to save him. She was no longer a powerless child. This time, she *could* make a difference.

Her lungs began to ache. Her muscles were sore. If she didn't turn around now, she might not make it back at all.

Come on! she screamed in the confines of her thoughts. It's me that you want. I'm the one who wouldn't go along with your plans, I'm the one who messed you over. Take me, not him. Me! Take *me,* damn you!

Suddenly, Kimberly was struck by something that might have been a fist, but something large enough to swat her entire body, driving what little breath she had left from her lungs. The force of the blow carried her upward. She was thrust from the waters, lifted into the air, and felt herself falling. She struck the surface of the waters and scrambled to gain control of herself. The waters tingled as if they had been charged with electricity.

Another figure floated beside her.

Griff! He was face down. Kimberly turned him over. His face was blue, his eyes wide, his mouth open in a scream.

"You're not dead," Kimberly chanted as she grabbed him and began to haul him back to shore. "You're not. You're *not dead.*"

As she swam back to the shore, dragging Griff with her, Kimberly fought the sudden increased violence in the waters. Winds emanating from the whirlpool pushed at her, driving her away from it, but the waters themselves twisted and churned, tugging at her.

As the shore approached, Kimberly saw that Ashlyn was lying on the ground in a crumpled heap. The Sentinel stood over her, its burning eyes glaring at Kimberly in open hatred. Two words suddenly flared in her mind: *You win.* The creature looked away. *For now.*

Suddenly, Kimberly saw a brilliant flash of light that seemed to be filtered through the most magnificent kaleidoscope imaginable. The waters rose up and parted, drenching the shoreline and all upon it. Screams unlike anything she had ever heard before echoed through the night. Then she was on the shoreline and it was over.

When Kimberly's senses cleared, she saw that the Sentinel was gone. In its place was a statuette that resembled it in perfect detail. It was clutched in Ashlyn's

186

hand. Kimberly did not need to check on Ashlyn to know the girl was dead. She had been dead for quite some time. She had finally stopped moving, that was all.

Griff!

Kimberly turned to see her boyfriend, lying on the shoreline beside her, his body turned from her. She saw no movement. Refusing to believe that he could be dead, Kimberly cried his name and turned him over. His face was relaxed. His breathing was shallow but regular. Suddenly, he opened his eyes.

They were violet and burning.

"You know who I am," Griff said in a voice that was not his own. *"Don't you?"*

When Kimberly did not answer, Griff shifted slightly, and suddenly another figure seemed to be occupying the same space that he did. A woman with auburn hair and violet eyes, wearing a luminous white dress.

"Victoria McConnel," Kimberly said. "Griff, is he—"

"He's fine. There isn't much time. Others will be arriving soon. You must listen."

Kimberly nodded.

"My body was destroyed, but my spirit survived. I took on the task of safeguarding this plane from the evil that nearly ruined my family centuries ago. But it's been a lonely existence. My soul has diminished in power over the centuries. Once I could easily have prevented the evil from escaping into the world. No more. My own selfish longing to spend eternity with my husband eroded my will. Once the beast was loose, my power was even less.

"Once your heart had been freed from the creature's evil, I was able to take the body of poor Ashlyn and help you. But it was your willingness to sacrifice yourself for the young man you loved that sent the beast back into its cage.

"I don't have the strength to carry on as the guardian. Someone has to watch over the beast and prevent it from ever again manifesting in the mortal realm."

"Why can't we destroy it?"

"It is undying. So long as there is evil and hatred in the world,

it survives. The best we can do is contain it. Will you be the guardian?"

Kimberly bit her lip. "What if I say no?"

"Then I hope you will at least find someone who will be agreeable to the task. My time is done."

Nodding, Kimberly watched as the spirit of Victoria McConnel separated from Griff. Another figure, vaguely male, appeared behind her, and enfolded her in its arms. They vanished, leaving no trace.

Griff moaned. In the far distance, Kimberly heard the wail of sirens. She leaned down and kissed Griff, then went to the body of Ashlyn McConnel. Prying her fingers loose from the statuette was not an easy task, but she accomplished it, then went deep into the woods and buried the statue before the police arrived. No matter what she decided, she could not allow it to fall into their hands. Then she returned to Griff and waited.

Soon, an officer appeared. It was Murphy, the young, dark-haired man who had arrested Griff.

Kimberly had no idea how she would explain any of this. If Ashlyn's earlier statement was true, Griff was about to be arrested for Gregory Rose's murder and there was nothing she could do to help him. She cradled Griff's head in her lap as the officer approached. Griff had not yet regained consciousness. When he did, there would be a lot to explain.

"You two are okay," Murphy said. "Thank God." Turning, he saw the body of Ashlyn McConnel. He bent down, checked her neck for a pulse, and hung his head. "It looks like she drowned."

Yeah, Kimberly thought, but who knows how long ago.

The officer turned his attention to Kimberly and Griff. "How's he doing?"

What do you care? Kimberly wanted to ask. You just want to make sure he's fit to stand trial, right?

"You want to tell me what happened?" he asked. "It looks like this one tried to drown you and your boyfriend got hurt saving you."

188

Kimberly had no idea where *that* scenario had come from, but she wasn't about to argue. "Yeah, sure."

The officer nodded.

"You're not going to arrest him?" Kimberly asked.

"What for? Your friend at the club gave me this." He took out a small microcassette player and hit the PLAY button. Ashlyn's voice came through the tiny speaker as she confessed to the murders of Gregory Rose and Sharon Cruise.

Jenny, Kimberly thought, squeezing her eyes shut in relief. She was certain the woman had had no such recorder on her person earlier this evening. But, then again, how could she be certain of anything?

"We've got warrants on McConnel's accomplices," Officer Murphy went on. "They disappeared from the club."

Disappeared? Kimberly thought. No, they would never be found. Victoria and Jenny had taken care of everything.

"I found your car sitting off by the bushes. If I hadn't, it might have been forever before I came across you two. Sit tight, I'm going to go call in for an ambulance."

Murphy departed. Kimberly waited until she could no longer hear his footsteps before she leaned down, pressed her cheek against Griff's, and allowed herself the luxury of tears.

About the Author

NICK BARON grew up in a small New England town not unlike Cooper Hollow, the fictional setting for *The Nightmare Club* series. His memories of living in Cooper Hollow's uncanny twin continue to inspire him. His hometown, like Cooper Hollow and every small town, had its dark side.

Nick now lives in Florida, where he writes horror and fantasy novels under another name. As a writer, his earliest influences were authors such as Ray Bradbury, Harlan Ellison, Stephen King, and Dean Koontz. Nick believes these writers stretch the boundaries of imagination and terror without losing the humanity and humor that people find within themselves in even the most chilling circumstances.

The author loves movies and has worked in television as a writer and director. Currently he is working on several new projects, including more books in *The Nightmare Club* series.

Nick likes to hear from readers. He, and everyone at *The Nightmare Club*, would enjoy knowing how you like the books, and what you'd like to read in future stories. Write to him c/o The Nightmare Club, Zebra Books, 475 Park Avenue South, New York, NY, 10016. If you would like a reply, please include a stamped, self-addressed envelope.

SNEAK PREVIEW!

Here is a special preview of the next *Nightmare Club*. *Warlock Games* by Richard Lee Byers is now available!

THE NIGHTMARE CLUB #3
WARLOCK GAMES
by Richard Lee Byers

When Mark McIntyre walked into the teen club, the place was jumping. Kids chattered happily, or spun around each other on the dance floor. In the side room, video games buzzed and wailed. One player must have messed up, because the guys clustered around him laughed and jeered.

Nobody said hi to Mark.

It made him feel so lonely that he almost turned around and left. But he knew he'd feel just as lousy sitting by himself in the dorm—or barracks, as the moron instructors called it—so he parked himself at the end of the bar in the back of the room. He figured he'd look less like a social reject perched on one of the stools than if he sat at a booth or table by himself.

The bartender—if that's what you called the person behind the bar, even if she wasn't serving alcohol—worked her way down to him. She was a pretty blonde, probably in her twenties, with big violet eyes. She gave Mark a smile that made him feel a little less down.

"Hi," she said. "I haven't seen you before, have I? I'm Jenny Demos. My father and I own the Night Owl Club."

Mark introduced himself.

"You must be a new cadet out at Hudson."

He'd changed out of his gray and navy-blue toy soldier suit before he had left the military academy, so for a second, he wondered how she knew. Then he remembered the haircut the school had made him get. He didn't quite look like a skinhead, but it was close. "Yeah," he sighed.

She lifted an eyebrow. "You don't sound too happy about it."

Mark shrugged. "It's a pain, being the new kid." He ought to know. His father's job made him move so often that Mark had gone to fourteen schools in ten years. And now, with Dad going to Paraguay, Mark had been dumped in the boarding school. He didn't even have his parents around anymore. As far as Mark was concerned, it was a bad joke to send him to an academy with the motto: "We teach leaders of men." He'd never been a leader. Heck, he'd never stayed anywhere long enough to be a follower! He'd always been a stranger, the outsider. "At least if you're the only new *junior.* The other new kids, the sophomore class, hang together, and the older guys hang with the friends they made last year."

Jenny nodded. "I know what you mean, because my dad and I used to travel a lot ourselves. For what it's worth, Cooper Hollow is . . . strange but nice, a thousand times nicer than some places I've seen. I'm sure you *will* make friends, if you just reach out. Did you want to order something?"

"I guess a Coke."

She poured one from the soda dispenser. "There you go. On the house." A boy at the other end of the bar waved an empty glass. "I've got to get back to work. I'll see you in a little while." She bustled away.

As Mark sipped the Coke, he decided that maybe Jenny had given him good advice. If he was lonely, he shouldn't sit and feel sorry for himself, he should try to meet someone. But who? He looked around the club.

And noticed the two girls sitting just a few feet away. One was tall, with frosted curls. The other was short and slim, with a pixieish face and silky brown hair. Somehow, the pair looked nice, not stuck up, and the smaller one was so pretty that Mark would have been interested in meeting her even if he'd already made a thousand friends. He

193

gulped the rest of his drink, pushed his glasses up his nose, got up, and walked over to their table.

"Hi," he said.

The girls looked at him.

He introduced himself. They just kept staring. He blundered on, feeling more awkward by the second. "I, uh, just moved here, and I don't know anybody, and I was wondering if I could sit with you."

The tall girl made a show of looking him up and down. "Well, you don't dress *too* dorky," she said at last. He felt himself redden. She sniffed. "And I don't smell any BO. But you've got that horrible, *horrible* hair, just like the rest of the Hudson Hitler Youth. I don't know if stylish ladies like us—"

"All right," Mark muttered, turning away.

"Wait!" said the pixieish girl. "She's only teasing. Of course you can sit with us. I'm Laurie Frank and my awful friend is Joan Adams."

Mark hastily took a chair. "Thanks. Uh, what school do you guys go to?"

"Cooper High," Laurie said. "And we know where you go. How do you like the Hollow so far?"

"I don't know yet," Mark said. "What do people do for fun around here?"

Laurie frowned, thinking. "Well, of course, there's here, the Nightmare Club . . ."

"I thought it was the Night *Owl* Club," Mark said.

"It is," Laurie said. "But everybody calls it the Nightmare Club because it looks so creepy from the outside. And because the building is supposed to be haunted."

Mark grinned. "Are you kidding me again?"

"Really, that's what the legends say," Joan said. "Probably because so many people have died here. In the late 1700s the place was a tavern where men met to fight duels. In the 1850s it was a stop on the underground railroad, but the couple that ran it went crazy, and tortured and murdered the runaway slaves. In the 1890s it was an orphanage, and a bunch of the children died in a fire. In the 1920s—"

"Don't *ever* give Joan a chance to show how much she knows about something," Laurie said, grinning. "She'll rattle on for hours."

"That's a cruel lie," the tall girl said, smiling back. "It's just that—"

"What are you doing with my sister?" a male voice growled.

Startled, Mark twisted in his chair. A beefy guy in a red and white Cooper High varsity jacket was glaring down at him. The newcomer had red, sunburned-looking skin and shoulder-length brown hair that he probably thought made him resemble a rock star. Acne spotted his square jaw.

Laurie scowled. "We're just talking, Barry. Chill before you embarrass yourself, okay?"

"I told you," Barry said, "I don't want you hangin' with guys from Hudson." He sneered at Mark. "Take a hike."

"Why?" Mark asked. "What's the problem?"

"I'm warning you," the hulking boy said. "Go." Kids at nearby tables began to gawk. Some stood up and moved closer.

"Forget it," Mark said. After all, what was Barry going to do about it, pop him in the middle of the teen club?

That was exactly what he did.

Mark was looking at the Cooper High student, but somehow he never saw the punch. One second he was sitting, the next, tumbling, the side of his face stinging. His glasses flew off, and his chair crashed to the floor.

The Hudson cadet scrambled to his feet and raised his fists. Grinning, another guy in a red and white jacket emerged from the mass of spectators, his silver skull earring glinting. "You're toast, rich boy," he said.

Mark's anger turned to fear, a sick, hollow feeling in his stomach. No way could he handle both Cooper High boys at once.

Then two other guys stepped out of the crowd to stand beside him. He was as surprised as he was relieved. He'd seen both kids at Hudson, but they'd never even spoken to

195

him.

"*Three* toy soldiers," Barry said. "Okay, no problem." He shuffled forward to strike. But Mark lunged first, swung, punched him in the gut and doubled him over.

A white-haired man with a beak of a nose shoved through the spectators. Mark guessed he must be Jenny's father. "Stop!" he bellowed.

For some reason, perhaps a trick of the room's acoustics, the shout split the air like a thunderclap. Stunned, the teenagers froze.

"If you fight in here, I'll see you in jail," the old man said, his gray eyes blazing. "If you fight on my *property*, I'll see you in jail. Get out. And don't come back until you learn to behave."

One of the cadets, a chunky, short-legged guy with Ross Perot ears, said, "These jerks started it."

"Out!" Mr. Demos roared. The kid with big ears flinched back. *"Now!"*

Mark hastily picked up his glasses. Then he and the other would-be fighters trudged to the exit, the crowd opening before them. Mr. Demos followed and stood on the stoop, no doubt to make sure they didn't resume their fight as soon as they stepped into the night.

Barry sneered at the cadets. "Next time."

"In your dreams," the chunky cadet said.

Barry flipped him off, then he and his friend strode down one of the paths into the woods that separated the Nightmare Club from the rest of Cooper Hollow. The kid with big ears turned to Mark. "McIntyre, right? I remember when Colonel Green introduced you at assembly. I'm Ken Wilson, and this is Greg Tobias."

Greg was tall and thin, with pale skin, black hair, and dark, deep-set eyes that made Mark think of an animal peeking out of a cave. In fact, the guy looked a little creepy, but Mark was too grateful to be put off. He held out his hand. "Thanks, both of you."

"Our pleasure," Greg replied, wrapping his long, white fingers around Mark's. For a moment, his hand felt cold and dry, but the next second, it seemed like anyone else's.

196

"We couldn't let those creeps hurt one of our own."

"I guess we might as well get out of here, too," Ken said. "Go back to the academy."

It occurred to Mark that if he waited, he might be able to talk to Laurie some more. Even though he'd only spent a minute with her, he really liked her. But Mr. Demos might not let him hang around until she came out. And if he walked back to school with Greg and Ken, maybe he could strike up a couple of genuine friendships. He could use some. "Sure, let's go," he said.

They set off down a path that ran to the north, their sneakers crunching the first fallen leaves. The sound echoed from the slopes around them. If Mark hadn't known better, he might have thought something was following them.

"So does anybody know what that garbage was all about?" he asked.

Ken said, "Townie guys hate cadets. Especially if we hit on townie babes."

Mark shoved a pine branch out of his path. The needles pricked his hand. "Why?"

Ken shrugged. "I don't know. Maybe because they think we look stupid playing army, which I guess we kind of do. Or because our families have enough money to send us to private school, and most of theirs don't."

"In other words, they're jealous," Greg said. "And they should be."

Ken said, "I don't know about that. But both years I've been here, there's been trouble. Fights. Practical jokes. That kind of stuff."

Greg smiled. "At orientation, the colonel told us new cadets to uphold Hudson's traditions, didn't he, Ken?"

"Yeah," Ken said.

"Then this year, why don't the three of us, and maybe some others we're sure we can trust, take care of the pranks?"

"I don't know," Ken said. "I cut some classes last year, and the instructors came down on me hard. I don't really want to get into more trouble this year."

"Come on," Greg said, "those townies tried to beat up Mark, two-on-one. We *owe* them. And it'll be fun. You're in, aren't you, Mark?"

Mark said, "I don't know." He didn't particularly want to get into trouble either, and perhaps because he'd managed to hit Barry back, he wasn't quite as mad anymore. "What—"

Greg's black eyes glittered, and Mark's head began to throb. Suddenly he was reliving the shock of being sucker-punched, and the stab of fear when the kid with the skull earring joined the fight. His rage surged back full force. "I mean, yeah, I'm in," he said.

"See?" Greg said. "*Mark's* not chicken." He gripped Ken's shoulder. "Come on, man. We need you. Besides, now you know too much. If you won't join the team, we'll have to kill you." He grinned. His long fingers squeezed.

A chill breeze gusted, and Mark shivered. A cloud oozed in front of the crescent moon. For a heartbeat, Ken's round face looked slack and dazed. Maybe it was a trick of the wavering light.

"Well . . . okay," the stocky senior said, blinking.

"Great!" Greg said. "You know, if we're forming a secret brotherhood, we ought to do it right. Like in the movies. Have tokens to show who belongs." He reached in his pocket and brought out two figurines.

Mark stepped closer to inspect them. They were wooden carvings the soft gray color of a Hudson uniform. One was a turreted tower, and the other was a warrior armed with a spear and shield.

"A rook and a pawn," Ken said. "You carry a chess set in your pocket?"

Greg said, "I like to play, so why not? From now on, carry these with you."

Mark thought the idea was kind of childish, but if it would make Greg happy, what the heck. He took the pawn, and Ken accepted the castle. "I guess we can call ourselves the Chessmen," the chunky senior said.

"I like it," Greg said. "And I think we should start our reign of terror tonight. Meet me on the rifle range an hour after lights out."

Mark crouched in the bushes beside the one-story brick building that was Cooper High. His palms were sweaty and his heart thumped. Greg's screwdriver scraped in the crack between the door and the jamb.

An hour earlier Mark had sneaked out of the dorm and down to the parade ground, where he saw that Greg had already recruited two more Chessmen. The tall, pale sophomore had passed out hammers, hatchets, pry bars, flashlights, and cans of spray enamel that he'd borrowed from the custodian's workroom, then the cadets hopped the wall and walked into town.

Slipping through the deserted streets had been fun, but once they reached Cooper High, Mark started getting nervous. After all, the cadets were trying to break into a public building. If somebody caught them, they'd be in real trouble. He wished they could give it up, but he wasn't quite willing to suggest it. He didn't want his new friends to think he was chicken.

"Why don't we bust a window?" Stan, a junior with a bristly red crewcut, asked. He sounded edgy; Mark was glad that at least he wasn't the only one.

"Somebody might hear," Greg said. "Or come along and see it afterward. I think I'm getting this, just keep your pants on." He murmured something under his breath. The door clicked. "There!" Gripping the handle, he pulled it open.

The cadets hastily trooped inside, into a locker-lined hallway. Flashlights clicked on. Circles of white light swooped about.

Greg pulled the door shut. "Don't make a lot of noise," he warned. "At least, not until we find something worth trashing."

"Right," said Warren, a wiry Asian sophomore. "But we can still let them know that we were here." He shook a can of paint, then wrote HMA RULES across four lockers. The hiss of the spray seemed loud in the stillness. The smell stung Mark's nose.

"Cool," Greg said. "But you ought to really dis them. Get personal."

Warren grinned. "You got it." He wrote a dirty remark about Cooper High girls, then drew a rude picture to go with it. Watching, Mark felt ashamed and excited at the same time. Ashamed because he didn't like the thought of a nice girl like Laurie having to see something so nasty, and excited because it was fun to be a part of something forbidden.

"Excellent," Greg said, slapping Warren on the shoulder. "Now let's go." The Chessmen proceeded farther into the school, Warren and Stan occasionally pausing to paint more graffiti.

Near the school's main entrance the cadets found an oil painting of pioneers building log cabins. On the wall opposite it was a display case crammed with plaques and trophies.

Greg said, "This is it."

Stan shook his paint can, then sprayed a four-letter word across the bottom of the painting. Greg tried to open the case, but the glass door wouldn't slide. Mark expected him to jimmy it, but instead he impatiently rapped it with the back of his fist. The glass shattered.

Ken gaped. "Jeez? Did you cut yourself?"

Greg smiled and held up his unmarked hand. "No." He reached into the case and pulled out a cup with a little bronze basketball player on top of it.

Mark didn't know he was going to speak until the word tumbled out of his mouth. "Wait!"

Greg frowned at him. "What is it?"

"Well . . . look. I wouldn't mind breaking up desks or something like that, because they can get more. But this picture and the trophies are different. They can't replace them."

"That's the point," Greg said. "We want to really tick them off."

"I know," Mark said, "but—"

Greg said, "Come on, man, don't wuss out on us. The

200

rest of us are only here because people messed with *you*. You still want to get even, don't you?" Even in the dimness, his dark eyes shone.

Something chilled Mark's thigh, as if the chess piece he held in his pocket had turned to ice. His head spun. When the dizziness passed, he was angry again. In his hand was a trophy topped with a symbolic atom—probably awarded for somebody's science project. He lashed it against the cinder-block wall. The base snapped off and fell to the floor. Mark dropped the cup and stamped it flat.

The other Chessmen cheered and started trashing the rest of the awards. Tools rose and slashed down. The chopping and hammering echoed.

In two minutes, all the trophies and plaques were ruined. Grinning, his chest heaving, Ken asked, "What's next?"

**Look for *The Nightmare Club's Warlock Games*
by Richard Lee Byers
Now on sale!**

**LOOK FOR A BRAND NEW SERIES COMING
IN OCTOBER 1993
SCREAM!**

SCREAM! books are an exciting, terror-filled thrill-ride. These skin-prickling page-turners will keep you on the edge of your seat, *screaming* for more!

WANTED TO RENT by Jessica Pierce

Sixteen year-old Christy Baker thinks it's totally unfair that her mother wants to rent out her bedroom to help make ends meet. But now Christy's really worried. There's something about their handsome boarder, Ethan Palmer, that gives her the creeps. Things get even creepier when she finds some strange things hidden in his bedroom. A coiled length of rope . . . a roll of masking tape . . . newspaper clippings about recently murdered women. *And* . . . a photo of herself!

Now Christy is home alone. The downstairs door has just opened. She knows who's come in — and why he's there!

BLOOD PACT by Debra Franklin

When Jamie Fox and her friends learn the abandoned train depot where they hang out is about to be demolished, they decide to take action. Forming a "suicide" pact, they sign their names in blood, vowing to kill themselves to keep the depot intact. Of course, they never really intended to carry out the pact . . .

Then, one by one, those who signed the blood pact, begin to die. The deaths are labelled suicides, but Jamie suspects her friends are really being murdered. Now she must unmask a cunning killer who's watching *her* every move. If she doesn't, she'll be the next to die!

DEADLY DELIVERY by Michael August

It's just another long, hot summer — until Derek Cliver and his friends join an exciting new mail-order club. The Terror Club allows Derek and his friends to create their own monsters. *And* it gives them the opportunity to "dispose" of those they despise most. But the game turns terrifyingly real when the monsters they create come to life — and actually murder their rivals.

Now, as the body count rises, Derek and his friends must somehow undo what they've done . . . before they become the next victims!

SCREAM!
BLOOD PACT
by Debra Franklin

His lips were getting closer. Jon Bon Jovi was about to plant an earthshaking kiss on her waiting mouth, which would undoubtedly transport her into an eternal state of bliss.

Then the telephone rang and woke her up. Jamie hated it when that happened.

Groping for the offending instrument on her nightstand, she hoped that whoever had cheated her out of such an excellent experience, even if it was just a dream (like she'd been aware of that minor detail until the stupid phone rang) would suffer the most hideous pimple breakout ever seen.

After mumbling a disgruntled hello into the mouthpiece, Jamie's left eardrum came under assault by the voice of her best friend Danica Hooker, whose Oklahoma twang immediately began blaring loudly and shrilly through the receiver, her words so jumbled and run together that Jamie could hardly understand a thing she was saying. Something about the newspaper.

Wincing, Jamie jerked the phone away and stuffed it under her pillow, sighed and silently counted out ten seconds (one, why me? — two, why me?) which she assumed would be long enough for Danica to run out of steam. Her timing had been correct. When she retrieved the instrument from under her pillow, Danica's voice had lost its hysterical edge and was now inquiring, "Jamie, are you

204

there? Did you go back to sleep? Jamie . . . ?"

Jamie groaned, stretching. "Danica, it's only eight-thirty. You know I like to sleep 'til noon on Saturdays, and you interrupted a really fantastic dream. I was just about to kiss—"

But didn't you hear me? Danica interrupted, her voice raising an octave. "Mayor Shepherd's going to tear down the old railroad depot and put in some stupid memorial statue and flower gardens with benches. And the demolition starts Monday after next!"

It took a few moments for the message to sink into Jamie's muddled brain, but when it did, she was jolted into full alertness. "Are you *serious?*" Springing upright, she tossed back a long tangle of strawberry blond hair which presently looked like a bird's nest.

"Go take a look at this morning's *Review*, it's right on the front page next to the article about Emma Parker breaking her leg." In a town of only thirty-five hundred such as Deer Creek, broken legs and just about everything else including disastrous home permanents were newsworthy.

Jamie was stunned. She, along with every other teenager in Deer Creek, felt a deep attachment to the abandoned railroad depot on the northwest side of town. It was and always had been their favorite hangout, a tradition handed down by their parents. Admittedly the dilapidated building was an eyesore even though it bore a fairly recent coat of red paint, but Jamie couldn't believe the mayor would even think of tearing it down. That old depot was as much an integral part of Deer Creek as the Town Hall, which wasn't exactly Caesar's Palace.

"We need to get together with the guys and talk about this," she said with an uncharacteristic note of determination. Jamie Fox was typically mellow (spelled l-a-z-y by her achievement-oriented father), not easily rattled by the winds of adversity—or Ds on her report card, like she by-God ought to be—but Danica's news riled her considerably. There had to be some way to keep the mayor from carrying out his plan. What's there to talk about. Danica responded sulkily. "We can't stop the mayor. Teenagers

205

don't have a voice in this stinkhole of a town."

"But we can't just sit back and watch it happen. We've at least got to try," Jamie insisted. "Listen, I'll pick you up in an hour. Call the guys and tell them to meet us at the depot."

"What am I, your secretary?"

Jamie expelled a heavy sigh into the mouthpiece, throwing her horrendous morning swamp breath back up at her. She winced. "Okay, you call Alan and Roman and I'll call Keith. Now g'bye." She depressed the cut-off button before Danica could think of any more testy comebacks. A few seconds later when she was rewarded with a dial tone, she started dialing Keith's number, but stopped midway and replaced the receiver in its aqua cradle. First she'd shower, brush her teeth and get dressed, then she would call Keith. That was just in case he had psychic powers he hadn't told anyone about, and that by listening to her voice he could receive an image of her, see what a wreck she was, sitting there wearing her dorkiest pair of pajamas. It was really a dumb notion and Keith was just a friend, but Jamie headed for the bathroom in the upstairs hallway anyway.

After showering and putting herself together, Jamie headed downstairs for breakfast. As she bounced into the kitchen she saw her mother looking up from the dining table in surprise, which was understandable, considering it was only nine-fifteen. It was common knowledge in the Fox household that Jamie always slept late on the weekends, and for at least an hour after getting up would drag herself around like a heavy sack of potatoes. If she did any bouncing, it would be off a door jamb or wall because she wasn't paying enough attention to where she was going.

Yet here she was up and dressed three hours earlier than usual for a Saturday and exuding an uncharacteristic amount of energy. Jamie could see a faint alarm going off in her mother's eyes.

"Something special going on, dear?" Gloria Fox asked casually.

Wanting to put her mother's fears that she was up to something sneaky to a rest, Jamie stalked up to the table and jabbed a finger at the newspaper folded to the cross-word section between her mother's forearms. "Didn't you read what Mayor Shepherd plans to do to the old depot? Danica said the story was on the front page."

Her mother reflected a moment in which her eyes took on a distant look, then she exclaimed with a smile, "Oh! That. Yes, well, the building's so old it's getting to be a danger, dear. Never know when it might decide to collapse, and someone — you, for instance — could get hurt. I think the flower gardens would be much better, don't you?"

Jamie was no longer a gullible child willing to accept any explanation given it. She'd done some thinking in the shower, and she was pretty sure she'd figured out the motivation behind Shepherd's plan. He was coming up for re-election pretty soon, and this time he had a contender, Malcolm Monroe. Monroe had lived in the area only a few years, but he'd brought a couple of businesses with him, businesses which had substantially improved Deer Creek's meager economy.

Monroe's son, Morey, attended her high school and he was in a number of classes with her. He was a major hunk who was popular with practically everyone in the school, especially the girls. Jamie was also no exception to his dark good looks and on more than one occasion, especially during a boring class, she had found herself wondering what it would be like to go out with him. probably all she would ever do was wonder. Morey tended to have a new girlfriend almost every month and he seemed to date only the most popular girls in school, especially those on the cheerleading squad. If there was one thing Jamie *wasn't*, or ever intended to be, it was cheerleading material. It was Morey's loss!

Gene Shepherd had been mayor of Deer Creek for twelve years, and he was very fond of the position. He would use every trick in the book and make up some new ones if necessary, whatever it took to hold his ground.

Tearing down the depot and erecting a scene out of Camelot was simply part of his re-election strategy.

"It's not as shaky as it looks, and anyway you said that was where Dad proposed to you. It wouldn't bother you at all to see it torn down?"

A gentle smile emerged on her mother's pale, careworn face. "I know how you feel, Jamie, but please, don't do anything that would embarrass your father. He's still hasn't quite gotten over that incident with Miss Frupp."

Miss Frupp was the secondary school's English teacher, and she had given Jamie an F on her essay titled "Small Towns/Small Minds," which Jamie had actually worked very hard on, at least by her standards. At any rate Jamie, and her friends, were of the opinion that the F was totally undeserved, but Miss Frupp refused to even discuss the issue, much less change the grade. Jamie then casually mentioned to Keith (who lived a few miles from town on a dairy farm) how fitting it would be if someone brought a stale cow pie to school and placed it in the seat of Miss Frupp's chair. Oddly enough someone did just that the very next day, and it went unnoticed by Miss Frupp until she sat down. Of course, by that evening every living soul in Deer Creek had heard the story. The old-timers who spent most of their empty hours in Ruby's Lounge thought it was a real hoot, and the juvenile set took great delight for weeks imitating Miss Frupp's expression during the moment of truth. Her father, however, had not been the least bit amused.

"What do you think I'm going to do, Mom? Chain myself to one of the depot's support pillars?"

"Oh, *heavens.*" Gloria Fox put a well-manicured hand to her collarbone. In the bright morning light pouring through the kitchen curtains, she looked every day of her thirty-eight years, a faded beauty queen with dark red hair and nothing much to do anymore except bake cookies for the church bazaars. "Jamie, don't even joke about doing such a thing, especially around your friends. One of them might think it was a good idea."

That was true, in fact it was right up Keith's alley. Jamie

could also picture him dressed in an army battle dress uniform, warding off approaching bulldozers with rotten egg missiles. "Don't worry, Mom. I was thinking more in the direction of a protest letter. That's allowable, isn't it? It is according to the Constitution, anyway."

Jamie smiled to herself, knowing that her mother could hardly argue against Constitutional rights. Her father probably would, but thankfully she wasn't dealing with him. Yet.

Gloria acknowledged defeat with a long sigh. "Would you like some bacon and eggs?"

"No time," Jamie said, turning to pull an unripe banana from the bunch sitting on the kitchen counter. "I'll just eat this on my way to Danica's. I told her I'd be there at nine-thirty."

"That banana's not much of a breakfast."

"I'm not very hungry," Jamie called back on her way out, leaving her mother sitting at the table shaking her head, a worried expression etched into her once-beautiful face.

Alan, Roman, and Keith had been waiting at the depot for almost twenty minutes by the time Jamie and Danica arrived in Jamie's new Corsica, which her father had gone to Elk City to buy. If you wanted to buy a vehicle in Deer Creek, you'd best be wanting a pickup, jeep, or tractor.

"Sorry we're late," Jamie apologized as she stepped onto the wide sagging porch where Keith and Roman were engaged in a rough game of rock-scissors-paper. Alan was perched on the railing, his lower lip bulging with chew, his reddened eyes indicating that he'd already started drinking. Both Alan's parents were alcoholics, and apparently he was following right along in their footsteps.

"My mom wouldn't let me leave until I cleaned up my room," Danica explained in a bitter tone. Wearing a frown, Danica's subtle attractiveness was replaced by the visage of an angry gnome with full cheeks, pug nose and frizzy light brown hair that hung almost to her rear. At five-one, she stood half a head shorter than the leaner, fairer-complected Jamie.

"And you should have seen it, looked like a war zone," Jamie added teasingly, taking note of the fact that Keith was looking at her rather strangely, as if he knew something she didn't. He was tall and lanky with shaggy brown hair and a boyish face, and on this late September morning he was wearing an oversized fuzzy blue sweater that made him look irresistibly cuddly.

"I've seen your room in worse condition," Danica countered.

Jamie shrugged. "My dad says I'm lazy, so I try not to disappoint him."

"So what are we gonna do about this place?" Alan piped up, then turned his head to eject a stream of brown spit. He was also tall but fairly thick around the middle, which was undoubtedly the result of all the liquor and beer he consumed on a daily basis. His parents hadn't yet noticed his pilfering, or if they had, didn't care enough to confront him. His hair was jet black, cheeks and upper lip darkened with manly stubble. His eyes, limpid pools of gray, appeared to be having trouble staying in focus.

"I say we kidnap the mayor's dog," Keith said, anxiously searching the faces of his friends for approval. Having met with only disparaging stares, he slumped against the slatted front wall of the depot. "It was just an idea."

Jamie flashed him a smile as she moved toward the depot's entrance, a pair of warped swinging doors lodged permanently inward. Each contained a dome-shaped glass window which constituted the only areas not covered with graffiti. "Yeah, and a really dumb one, Keith. Try thinking of something we could say in a letter that would make him change his mind."

Stepping over the threshold onto heavily scuffed black and white linoleum, Jamie gazed nostalgically at the inner walls, also covered with familiar graffiti. DARREN + BOBBI JO = LUV 4-EVER—1957. LONG LIVE ELVIS THE PELVIS. SHAYNE TIDWELL LOVES RITA HAINES—1974. LET IT BE. MOTLEY CRÜE PARTY ON DUDES—SF'89. Jamie thought the graffiti alone made the old depot a very special place. A lot of sentiment had been scratched, painted, or penned on these walls, and though most of it was inane, it still displayed in its unique way the changing of generations, each marching to its own drummer. It was sort of like a museum. Maybe if the mayor could see it from that perspective, he'd leave it alone and find some other way to polish his image.

The others had followed her inside. Alan teetered over to one of the long wooden benches and dropped ungracefully onto it, making a sloshing sound that indicated he had a bottle or flask stashed somewhere on his person, probably in one of the pockets of his pea coat. Danica slowly wandered over to the abandoned oak ticket counter, looking everything over as if for the last time.

Keith came up behind Jamie and wrapped his arms around her, which made her jump slightly. "I got it," he said, bending down to rest his chin on her right shoulder. "We write the mayor an anonymous letter threatening to kidnap his dog. He brags about her being the best hunting dog in the county, so that oughta make him think twice."

Jamie was confused by Keith's sudden display of affection, but she didn't try to move away in fear of hurting his feelings. It wasn't as if they hadn't hugged before, but there had always been a good reason for doing it. Celebrating the stroke of midnight on New Year's Eve, for instance, or when one of them had a birthday.

"Keith, would you please forget about the mayor's prize hunting dog. Since when do would-be kidnappers send an advance letter of warning? All Shepherd would think after receiving a letter like that is how to go about keeping his dog safe."

Roman turned from writing *I found it and turned it over to the sheriff* under the anonymous inscription *I lost my virginity here*. "What about a hunger strike? Maybe we could get all the kids in town to go on a hunger strike until the mayor reneges. I know my mom would be on his back day and night. She goes nuts when she thinks I'm not eating right." Her concern was understandable; since early childhood Roman had looked as if he'd been scrounging meals out of garbage cans. His skin always had a sickly pallor, and he was hands-down the scrawniest male senior at Deer Creek

Heritage Academy, a fact that made him a frequent victim of the redneck jock squad. His eyes, large pale blue marbles sandwiched between thick white-blond lashes, peered out from behind gold wire-rimmed glasses that matched his flat top. "Well? Is that a great idea, or what?"

Alan belched. "Or what, I'd say. I for one am very fond of eating, and I refuse to starve on account of this heap. Let's all get drunk at my place and just forget about it."

"Not me," Jamie said resolutely. "I don't want this heap to go down." Keith still had his arms around her, and she was beginning to wonder if he was actually coming on to her. The idea was almost laughable, as long as they had been friends. She could vaguely remember the two of them building castles and tunnels in her sandbox and catching tadpoles down at the crrek with his mother's tea strainer.

"I stand with Jamie," he said, choosing that moment to end the embrace and move a few paces away. Staring in the direction of the back wall where someone had painted a life-sized buck and doe posed peacefully at a stream, he crossed his arms over his chest. Maybe this a a heap, but it's our heap. Where else are we or any of the other kids our age going to hang out? The stupid skating rink?"

"My place," Alan said, spitting tobacco juice on the floor. "Always got plenty of booze. And entertainment, too. None of you have ever seen my parents really get into it, have you?"

"Get real, Alan," Danica smirked.

Having finished his witty contribution to posterity, Roman straightened up and thoughtfully tapped the end of his pen against his temple. Looking at him, Jamie found herself wondering where life's road would lead Deer Creek's little "Girly Man," as the jocks called him. Certainly he would not be returning here after graduating from Purdue, the Ivy League university at which he'd been accepted. Whatever direction he took, he would probably go far, she decided. The underdogs often did, while their persecutors ended up eking out a mediocre existence. In the long run, beauty and brawn didn't matter

212

very much. In the long run it was brains that counted, and Roman certainly had plenty of those. Surely a stroke of genius was gestating beneath that scrub brush he called hair.

Just then a slow smile began spreading across Roman's face, the kind of smile that always accompanied a gem of an idea. Jamie smiled back at him. "Okay Roman, what's your idea?"

Roman's smile widened. "Drum roll, please."

"For Chrissakes, just spit it out," Alan grumbled, leaning over to spit more tobacco juice on the floor.

Danica glared at Alan. "What's your problem? Maybe his idea deserves a drum roll. Like yours deserved unanimous raspberries."

"Chill out, you two," Jamie sighed. "If we start arguing, we're never going to get anywhere." Turning back to Roman she placed a hand on her hip and said, "Cut the suspense and just spit it out, Roman."

All eyes were on him. Roman let a few heartbeats of silence pass for added effect, then raised his arms in a gesture that said "here it is, a piece of cake, you simpletons" and opened his mouth to release one word.

"Suicide!"

The others' mouths fell open, but they were too stunned at first to say anything. Jamie could hardly believe what she'd heard. And she'd actually believed Roman had brains. He'd just proven that he had the intelligence of a weather vane.

Alan was first to speak. "Oh, now that's a brilliant idea, alright. I refuse to starve myself, but I have no problem at all with killing myself. So how should we do it? I've heard carbon monoxide poisoning is a nice way to go, you just fall asleep permanently, but that's not very dramatic. I say we should all climb to the top of the water tower and dive off."

"Roman! You are only joking, aren't you?" According to her anguished facial expression, Danica was more than simply surprised or shocked. Hugging herself and shivering as if suddenly cold, she stared at Roman with wide, pleading eyes.

"Of course he's joking," Keith said, but a look of uncertainty crossed his face. "Aren't you?"

Roman shook his head slightly and chuckled. "Come on, peeps, you know I'm not that stupid. I didn't mean that we should *do* it, just that we should *threaten* to do it. You know, send a letter like Jamie said, telling the mayor that if he continues with his plan to tear this place down, the five of us will kill ourselves. And we'll all sign it in our own blood, so it'll look like we really mean business. If that won't stop him, nothing will."

Jamie felt her smile returning as her faith in Roman's intelligence revived. He was absolutely right. His plan, though low-down and dirty, was their best shot. The mayor couldn't take the chance of having the citizens of Deer Creek think him indirectly responsible for their untimely deaths.

As far as she could see, there was only one drawback. There existed a strong possibility that word of the letter would get around, and in its journey through the small-town grapevine reach her father's ears. Undoubtedly this would come under the heading of social embarrassment in his book, but was it her fault that he shared the same sense of humor allotted to drill sergeants and grizzly bears?

"I think that's a great idea, Roman. If my dad finds out I'll probably lose my car keys for a month, but it'll be worth the sacrifice. Still, let's at least try to keep this a secret."

Keith nodded. "Sounds okay to me, except for the part about writing our names with our own blood. Can't we just dip our quills into a raw steak or something? I kinda doubt the mayor's going to send the letter off to a lab to have the blood analyzed."

Alan pulled a pint bottle of peppermint Schnapps from one of his inner coat pockets and twisted off the cap. "Gotta hand it to you, Romano, you come off with a pretty good one now and then. Let's have a drink to celebrate." He closed his tobacco-stained lips around the mouth of the bottle and tipped it straight up, chugging several hearty

214

swallows. Lowering the bottle he then held it out to Jamie.

"No thanks," she said.

They all declined in turn. Alan shrugged and proceeded to polish off the bottle himself.

"We need to get this done right away, before a ball starts rolling that not even the mayor can stop, like a signed contract," Jamie said, noticing uncomfortably that Keith was giving her that strange look again. "If we hurry, we can get it to the mayor's office before it closes at noon. I think I've got some notebook paper in my glove compartment."

"Good, now all we need is a raw steak. Anyone think to bring one along?" Danica quipped as she casually sauntered in Roman's direction with her hair pulled over one shoulder, hands jammed in the pockets of her jeans. For the first time Jamie noticed that Danica was starting to get a little pudgy around the middle. But that wasn't much of a surprise, considering her fondness for chocolate and sweets.

Jamie looked around at the others. Danica and Roman had retreated to a back corner where they were talking very quietly. They'd been doing a lot of that lately, and Jamie suspected there was something more intimate than friendship going on between the two, but for some reason neither of them would admit it.

"If everyone agrees, we'll spin Alan's bottle," Jamie said, her eyes flitting from face to face. "The one the neck points to gives the blood. That sound fair?"

After several seconds of meditative silence, everyone agreed. They gathered in a circle in front of the ticket counter, generously spaced. Jamie had taken charge of the bottle, since Alan was having a hard enough time just standing up straight. Stepping forward, she crouched in the center and laid the bottle on its front side.

"Well, here goes." She sent the bottle into a fast spin and quickly stepped back to her place, watching the revolutions as her friends were — with great trepidation. None of them were great lovers of pain.

"Please don't point at me," Roman implored aloud. "If my Mom sees a cut on my finger, she'll probably rush me

215

up to the hospital in Elk City for massive antibiotic infusions."

"We'll send a card," Keith grumbled.

Round and round the bottle went, slowing, slowing . . .

Danica stopped biting her lower lip long enough to say, "What is the unlucky winner supposed to cut him or herself with? A rock or a rusty tin can?"

"No way," Alan said with an adamant shake of his head. "I got my hunting knife up under the seat of my pickup, and I guarantee that baby is *shaaa-arp.*"

"Oh. I feel so much better now," Danica muttered sarcastically.

The bottle made its final revolution and pointed directly at Jamie. She groaned loudly. Danica, Roman and Alan simultaneously sighed with relief, then Alan stumbled back to the nearest bench. Stretching out horizontally, he complained that he didn't feel so good.

Keith, suddenly a white knight, raised the spirit of dead chivalry, startling them all, except for Alan, who was too busy getting sick. "I'll do it for you, Jamie. It's no big deal to me."

Jamie squinted at him. This from the same boy who'd not so long ago laughed his butt off when she stumbled barefoot into a sticker patch? Who, when swimming in the creek, liked to drop live crawdads down the back of her bikini bottoms? Who'd teased her relentlessly for getting scared when they'd all gone to Elk City to see the movie "Candyman"?

"Thanks, Keith, but the bottle pointed to me fair and square. Besides, it's no big deal to me either." *What are you saying?* an inner voice squealed. *You hate the sight of blood, especially your own! And you've been known to cry over paper cuts!*

"What a woman," Danica smiled.

Roman paused in the midst of counting his lucky stars. "What an idiot, you mean."

Jamie silently agreed with Roman. "Well, I'll go get the paper out of my glove compartment. Alan, you—" She looked toward the bench and saw that Alan had passed out.

"—have a nice nap," she finished lamely, shaking her head and feeling very sorry for him. He came off as being the happy-go-lucky type, but he had to be totally miserable behind that facade, or he wouldn't drink so much. He joked constantly about his parents and their knock-down, drag-out fights, but down deep, those bitter, drunken feuds were surely tearing him apart.

"I'll get the knife while I'm at it," she sighed, and headed for the door. Behind her she heard Roman say to Danica, "Go with her to make sure she doesn't try to make a run for it."

"Very funny, Roman," Jamie called out without looking back.

She returned a few minutes later with a sheet of notebook paper and Alan's hunting knife still in its sheath. She was in no particular hurry to have a look at the *shaaa-arp* blade.

Roman, Danica, and Keith had seated themselves on the opposite end of the front row bench where Alan was now snoring loudly.

Jamie handed the sheet of paper to Roman. "Here, it was your idea, so you compose the letter."

Silently Roman took the sheet of paper over to the scarred ticket counter and laid it down. After staring into space for several moments, he took the ballpoint pen from his shirt pocket and began to write. Jamie lowered herself on the bench between Keith and Danica.

"I wish you'd give me the knife."

Jamie glanced over at Keith, finding he had that weird moonstruck look in his eyes again. And for the first time in their long-standing relationship, Jamie looked back at him as a potential boyfriend instead of a regular friend, just to see how it would feel. She decided it felt very strange.

"I'm a big girl now, Keith. I can take it."

"For God's sake, let him do it," Danica said, nudging Jamie with her elbow. "What are you, some kind of masochist?"

Jamie's jaw set. "The bottle pointed to me, so I should do it. If it had pointed at you, I doubt if Roman would have offered to take your place."

"You doubt right," Roman muttered from across the rectangular, boxcar-sized room. His statement was punctuated by a hog-like snort from Alan.

"I'll remember that, Roman Alexander," Danica swore, her eyes narrowed into angry slits.

Definitely, there is something going on between those two, Jamie thought. But if they wanted it to remain a secret, far be it from her to blow the trumpet. Living in a small town was, to her, too much like living in a fish bowl as it was; privacy was a rare commodity. For sure she had faults, a few little ones, actually very tiny, itty bitty minuscule ones, but having a long nose to stick into other people's business was not one of them.

"So what's with you, anyway?" Danica asked, bending forward to address Keith with an arched eyebrow. "Would you have offered to step in for me, too, or have you finally been smitten by the love bug?"

Jamie gasped. "Danica! Get real."

Roman stopped writing and smiled in their direction. "First comes love, then comes marriage—"

Danica suddenly burst into tears.

Lips tightly compressed, Roman quickly turned back to the letter.

Jamie didn't know what to do or to think, but she had the sensation of being in over her head. Way over. An ugly suspicion arose. She pushed it back down. It rose again. Again she pushed it down. Danica was in some kind of physical pain, she firmly decided. Maybe her appendix had just ruptured or something. She placed her hand on Danica's shoulder.

"Are you in pain? Do you need to get to a doctor or hospital?"

Still sobbing, Danica adamantly shook her head.

Jamie looked to Keith. He shrugged, his expression clearly indicating that he didn't want to be dragged into it, whatever it was.

"Okay everybody, listen up," Roman announced briskly as he turned from the counter with the sheet of paper in his hands, acting as though nothing at all were amiss. "To whom it may concern. The old railroad depot may be an eyesore to some people, but to us it is a cherished resort, the only place where we can go and just be ourselves. It is also a nostalgic monument, its sentiments crafted by the hands of three generations. We will permit its destruction over our dead bodies. We mean this quite literally. We have made a pact, sealed by our own blood, that we will kill ourselves if the depot is destroyed. Signed . . ."

Roman looked up from the paper. "Well, how was that? Too sophisticated?"

Danica had stopped crying, but she still wouldn't look up. Jamie had been so concerned about her friend — and ticked at Roman for being such an insensitive clod — that she'd hardly heard any of it. So she gazed back at him but said nothing.

"Sounded fine to me," Keith said, his voice sounding small in the overwhelming silence.

Alan mumbled something unintelligible, then farted explosively.

This broke them all up, even Danica, who immediately scooted as far from Alan as she could get without climbing into Jamie's lap. Their boisterous laughter awakened Alan, who groggily pushed himself into an upright position looking like he'd just gotten off the Tilt-O-Whirl at the county fair after a ten-hour ride.

"What's e'rybody laughing at?"

"Your speech," Roman answered almost straightfaced, then burst into another maniacal peal with Keith and the girls. By now Jamie was laughing so hard that tears were coursing down her cheeks. Seldom did she witness perfect justice, but this was definitely one of those rare occasions.

Alan was obviously having a hard time keeping his eyes focused. "What, was I talking in my sleep?"

"Loud and clear," Keith chuckled, and to demonstrate exactly what he meant, pinched his nostrils together. Although Alan probably had the cognitive abilities of a rubber duck at the time, he got the picture, and his face blossomed red down to his collarbone.

"Quit laughin' or I'll do it again. Right in your face!"

"In your dreams!" Keith shot back, but he did stop laughing, as did Jamie and Danica. Roman was obviously trying very hard to get it under control, but every few seconds a snicker escaped as he silently reread the letter he'd composed.

Jamie mused at how quickly and easily normalcy—if such a term could be applied to a group of teenagers—had been restored. All it had taken was a fart. Yet it wasn't the same as before. And she had the feeling it would never be the same again.

Still smirking, Roman lowered the letter and fixed his eyes on Jamie. "I think this'll work. All it needs now are our bloody autographs."

Jamie winced at the hunting knife in her lap. Too bad this couldn't wait until the next time she shaved her legs—then everyone in the county could write their names. Slowly, with trembling hands, she undid the snap and pulled the heavy blade from its leather sheath. It shiny surface gleamed menacingly, promising exquisite pain.

"You'd better be careful or you'll cut your whole finger off with that thing," Danica cautioned.

Jamie's face paled. "I can't do it. Somebody else has to do it for me. And whoever wants the job better hurry before I chicken out or faint. I feel a little of both coming on."

"Oh, give me the knife, I'll do it," Danica said, a little too enthusiastically, Jamie thought. She reluctantly handed the knife over, then stuck out the forefinger of her right hand and tightly squeezed her eyes shut, her lips pulled back in a grimace.

"Not too deep. I don't want you coming at me next with a regular sewing needle and thread."

Danica took hold of Jamie's extended finger, and Jamie tensed. Danica's hand was a little shaky, too, she realized, which made her even more nervous. Terrible images flashed in her mind. Her mother taking one look at her and shrieking, "Jamie! Where is your right hand?!" But that was a bit extreme, hardly a real possibility. Hurry hurry hurry, she thought. However, lying on a hospital bed in the intensive care unit receiving massive transfusions to replace the gallon of blood she'd lost from the cut on her finger, now *that* she could see. In full technicolor detail.

"Come on, get it over with before I lose my nerve."

Danica surprised her by answering, "Relax, Jamie. It's already done."

Jamie could hardly believe it; she hadn't felt a thing. Gathering her courage, she opened her eyes to see how badly she was bleeding. But she wasn't. At all. What . . . ?

Looking up, she saw that Keith was now holding the knife, and there was blood dripping from a small cut on his left forefinger.

"I cheated," he said with a triumphant smile. Before she could get on his case about it he returned his gaze to the wound and called out commandingly, "So come on, people, let's do it. This isn't Old Faithful."

Jamie stared at him with mixed emotions. She was a little angry that he didn't allow her to perform her rightful duty, but then she was also grateful he'd cared enough to do it for her. Maybe he was trying to make up for all those crawdads, laughing at her ooching and owwing in that sticker patch. Her mind refused to speculate further, but she suspected that later she would probably open up to her diary, as she usually did.

Roman had taken his ballpoint pen apart so they could use the open end of the ink dispenser as a quill. One by one, grim-faced and mute, they dipped the pseudo quill into the blood pooled around Keith's wound and signed their names. Jamie was last to sign, and as she watched her friends commit their names in blood to the paper, an inexplicable, eerie feeling stole over her, as if what they were doing was for real, as if they were actually signing their own death warrants. It caused a quiet shudder to run through her, and she had no doubt that some heavy-duty nightmares were forthcoming.

"Your turn, Jamie." Danica was offering her both the letter and the thin plastic cylinder, its hollow tip crimson with Keith's blood. Swallowing a sudden lump in her throat, Jamie took them from her and added her name to the list.

**LOOK FOR *BLOOD PACT* ON SALE EVERY-
WHERE IN BOOKSTORES IN OCTOBER 1993!**